Published by Red Giant Entertainment
(www.RedGiantEntertainment.com)
an imprint of Active Media Publishing, LLC,
614 E Hwy 50 #235 Clermont, FL 34711 USA.
Benny R. Powell, President. David Campiti, Creative Director.

Book design by Susan Mangan.

ISBN 978-0-9848808-0-5
Printed in China.
First Printing

10 9 8 7 6 5 4 3 2 1

MEDUSA'S DAUGHTER

written by Jonathon Scott Fuqua

story by Steven Parke
and Jonathon Scott Fuqua

RED GIANT ENTERTAINMENT

For Calla… Your dazzling temperament and internal and external beauty—all combined with your incredible theatrical and artistic sensibilities—consistently belie the fact that you are my sweet daughter. I hope the world and those whom you care for always provide you with a great soft embrace. I will always love you.
—*Jonathon Scott Fuqua*

To my mom and dad who have relentlessly supported me through all kinds of crazy ideas, and to my son who inspired me to let my stories out.
—*Steven Parke*

CALL ME MAIA.

I'm not normal.

I never have been.

My heart and even my dreams tell me I'm capable of terrible, unhuman acts, though human is what I most want to be.

Those who have worked for Rictus Fitch over the last decade have born witness to my troubles. They know the things I've done. But they can't fear me any more than I fear myself. Because it is my sad circumstance, not theirs, to live inside my head.

Call me Medusa's Daughter.

In Greek mythology, Medusa was one of the three hideous Gorgon daughters of the gods Phorcys and Cito. Her hair was like constrictor snakes, her teeth and skin like those on of a crocodile. She was so awful looking that her gaze turned anybody who looked at her to stone.

It was Perseus, a hero from Greek mythology, who cut her head off as she slept. He thankfully rid the earth of her forever. Or, that is, until now. I'm said to be her daughter, which, due to all the years in between, is impossible. It's more likely I'm a descendant.

Besides, there are some obvious differences between me and the original Medusa. She had snakes on her head. I've got hair. And after Perseus severed Medusa's neck, out lept Pegasus, the beautiful white winged horse. Following it, sprang a giant named Chrysaor. I like to remind myself of that, because if something happened to my neck, I'm sure that a winged horse and a giant wouldn't jump out. It sounds stupid, but there's not nearly enough room inside of me. I've got a skinny neck, and I'm sort of thin.

Then again, Medusa existed in myth. And mythology, Rictus often says, "is merely an attempt by the naïve, such as yourself, to explain what they don't understand. The stories of Medusa and her sisters are likely just a way to explain something that was hard to believe."

I frequently nod back.

"Personally," he'll go on, "I believe Gorgons were just failed freaks of evolution. Disgusting mutations, basically." He smiles. "That makes you a mistake, dear," he has told me more than once.

And why, you ask, would I believe anything that Rictus Fitch says?

It's simple. I have no choice. Also, he saved my life as surely as the doctor who delivered me lost his own. Rictus explains it this way, "The man delivered you and as your eyes opened his closed. His heart stopped as soon as he got a good look at you."

"And… and… your hideous parents, freaks themselves, were so upset by what they had created that they tried to drown you in the Aegean Sea. And why not? Those islands had seen your like before, Medusa's Daughter, and nobody wanted to be visited by a creature such as you again."

"It was no more than luck and circumstance that I came upon your disgusting parents in the act of the atrocity, known to the world as infanticide, that would've been your drowning."

Apparently, my parents, my family, left me to die on a famous rock that resembled a winged foot at low tide and was submerged at high. It was there that at great risk to his own life, Rictus says he saved me. Except, I've never seen Rictus risk his life for anything or anyone, ever. In a pinch, I'm not even sure he could save himself.

Today, I am standing beside him and dying to ask him a question that he won't like. Finally, unable to wait for the right moment, I say, "Rictus, sir, are you sure you plucked me from that rock?"

"What rock?"

"The one shaped like a winged foot. Are you sure someone else wasn't responsible for saving me from drowning when I was a baby?"

Furious, he meets my eyes. "Yeah, I am, girl."

"But, sir… the other night I overheard you tell someone that you can't even tread water. I heard you say that."

"So?"

"Then how'd you swim through the crashing waves, like you said?"

He stares at me harshly. "Did it with my wits."

I nearly smile, which would have been a terrible mistake. I want to say, "Do your wits float?" But I know better than to be a smart-aleck with him. Once, Lulu, "the World's Smallest Woman," was rude to him, and Rictus renamed her "the Human Monkey," and made her play like she was a bald chimpanzee with a girl face for two months. Lulu hated doing that, too, especially because it required that she paste clumps of hair from an Angora goat to her face, arms, and legs before every show. Since then, she decided to leave the festival, and I don't blame her.

Rictus brushes his square-tipped fingers across his stubble. "Maia, I risked everything I have to save a baby that had only just murdered its first sad victim. I can't explain the goodness that drove me through those treacherous waves anymore than I can explain God in Heaven, but I saved you, Medusa's Daughter. Are we clear on that?"

"Yeah," I say, but I know he's a liar. I've heard him lie to others, so I know he lies to me.

"Good."

He tells me that I'm obligated to him, that I owe him with my life because he risked his own to save me. I wonder how long I'll have to work in his sideshow before I've repaid him, though. I worry he'll keep me here till my fingers are swollen with arthritis or my eyes hardly work anymore.

Besides, maybe Rictus is right about me. Where would I live? Girls my age spend most of their day in school learning about the world and math, which is how to combine numbers in different ways other than the normal adding and subtracting. I don't even know why that would be useful. Also, I don't know anything about the world except about Europe and how Mount Everest is the highest mountain and if I lived in America and dug straight through the earth, I'd come out in China, where people look like Kytanno, one of the ladies who used to work the card tables. Actually, I know more than that, but I can't think of more right now. Being uneducated and unnatural like I am, would I ever survive the real world? The question gnaws at me the same way tiny minnows pick at fish bait dangling in the water from a hook.

I wonder if normal girls have so many problems. I bet they don't. First, I hope their parents didn't try to drown them in the sea on the day they were born, and second, there's only one Rictus Fitch in the world, thank God for everyone. I also bet regular girls can speak the language of the countries they live in and that they don't spend hours everyday in a tiny animal cage with straw in the bottom and a drinking bowl to sip from. Also, I bet when they were young they weren't terrified of themselves, which was pretty stupid of me but is true.

I'm not precisely sure, but I think my nervousness of me started because of what I did every single day. Visitors to the festival arrived to gawk and holler in my face, like they do now except I was younger. They treated me like I had a monster inside my skin waiting to burst free. At night, I felt like I was sleeping inside the body of a terrible killer. I grew terrified that as I slept in my tiny silver trailer my hair might somehow strangle me or crawl out with me behind it and choke someone else. That's why I began trying a series of unhelpful things to keep myself and others safe.

When I was six, I remember borrowing scissors, bolt cutters, and even a World War Two soldier's knife from the giant carnie tool chest. With them, I tried to hack my locks off. I chopped, cut, and sliced, and all three tools grew more and more dull. Plus, it hurt. I never realized that my hair was like a part of my body, like another set of fingers or a patch of wavering arms. I never realized it could feel.

After that, I decided to be more preventative. After leaving my cage for the evening and washing dirt and grease pencil from my face and arms, I'd prepare for bed by carefully wrapping each clump of my hair with strands of metal wire that I tied off and fastened to a small steel ring mounted to the metal steps of my trailer. When I was done, I scooted away as far as I could, till my hair pulled tight, then I curled up and slept on the floor. It went like that for a few months, until I woke up and found that the metal ring was stretched open and the wires holding down my hair, every single one of them, were shredded so that they resembled silver stalks of wheat unraveling.

After that, I gave up on the steel ring idea and started wrapping my head before bedtime. I used thick, striped pieces of old tent canvas and heavy tie-down rope to create what looked like a straight jacket or sausage casing starting just above my eyes. It was hard to do, and actually took longer than my old trick of anchoring my hair down. But, it seemed worth it. And it was, at first. It worked for a little more than four weeks before I woke up early in the morning in a dream where I was attacked by people who worked in a fish market, only to find the rope severed and frayed, the heavy canvas torn into small strips.

For a few days after that, I carried around a pencil and paper and drew all sorts of hair holding and binding contraptions, but I never tried to build another one. Over a week or so, I decided that if my hair wanted to hurt me, I couldn't stop it.

Nine years have passed since then. I'm fifteen now. My hair has never done a thing violent to me except once when we were both being playful with Skelly and a lock snapped like a whip at his hand but caught my chin instead, splitting it pretty good. That was just a small, regular mistake, though. In all of our lives, we've only committed one large one, and that was forever ago now. It can't count anymore. I hope.

Still, I've begun to worry that soon I'll be capable of large and totally irregular mistakes that could affect more than just my life.

It rained earlier. The air is still warm, but it's not heavy. From behind my dark, dark glasses, I stare at the crowd, which has backed away. I lock onto the worried eyes of a boy much younger than me. I crawl forward, doing my best to look like an enormous, menacing spider, my fingers splayed, my toes dirty. Above, my hair fans outwards and touches the ceiling and edges of my cage like dark water defying gravity. It's strange, but when my hair is alive and moving, it seems to grow in length and thickness. It becomes threatening. Peering over my shoulder is a painting of the real Medusa, her wicked face laughing, her hair replaced by huge snakes with snapping jaws. She is scaly, and her eyes bulge hideously. She's supposed to bear some resemblance to me.

The boy studies the painting, then me. His nose is small, turned up. His face is round, his hair falling across his smooth forehead. Back and forth his eyes go, from me to the Medusa poster. I wonder what he's thinking. I don't know. I can't ever predict what young boys might do because it seems like they might do anything. Half run away. Others stay. A few get closer. A handful throw rocks or bottles at me.

I wonder where his parents are and if they've abandoned him the way mine abandoned me on the winged-foot rock. That causes me to wonder if he can move his hair, which is a stupid thing to wonder since it's so short. Still, I want to ask.

But I know not to speak. Rictus punishes anyone who breaks character. Lulu the midget, who'd sung songs and had conversations with guests when she was the World's Smallest Woman, wasn't allowed to say a word once she became the Human Monkey. Nobody is allowed to be their real self during working hours unless their real self is part of the show.

Skelly, my best friend, walks up behind the boy and smiles at me. He's the festival's loud mouth or what people who work in carnivals know as a shill. He's the presenter of the show, the ringmaster, except we don't have rings.

Skelly kneels down and puts an arm around the boy. Clearing his throat, he shakes the kid softly, and I notice the boy's nose wrinkle when he gets a load of Skelly's alcohol breath. It's the same thing mine does when I'm around him. Skelly says, "A terrible sight, eh, young mister?"

The boy points at the banner behind me. "Yeah. She's ugly, but not like the painting. That's… really scary."

"Oh, you're right. You're right about that. But this one here in front of us, she's still young and has room to grow and change. Gorgon's, which Medusa's Daughter happens to be, they gets worse with age. Much worse."

The boy shivers. "Why is she wearing sunglasses?"

"'Cause, boy, one look into her angry eyes and you're dead. Stone. Calcified as a fossil. One look into her eyes, and she'll turn ya straight to rock."

The way his bottom lip begins to quiver, I can't help but think of an earthquake, a tiny one that affects only his face. "How close can I get before she can grab me?"

"Ya can touch the cage, but ya gotta be real careful. She's a conniving little neck breaker. She wants to draw ya in and take ya down hard. Oh, I seen it happen. There was a child lost his hand once."

The boy tightens his fingers about the links of my cage. "She's so dirty?"

"Ah, yes she is. We can't clean her is why. Not unless one of us wants to risk our lives. Did I say them fangs she's got is horrible infectious, too?"

"No."

"They is."

"She looks so… kind of normal."

"Oh, lad, I been here watching the monster for about an hour now. I seen her way. She ain't calm. Watch this." Skelly takes his cane, holds it loosely in a veiny hand, then bangs the links of my cage with the tip.

I hiss at him loudly. I pretend to reach for the child.

Skelly pulls him back to where I can't grab him, at least that's what they think.

"Did… did she try and hurt me?" the boy asks, his poor eyes swollen like two German coins.

"I believe she did, child. But I can't read her mind."

The boy turns and runs through the crowd of people who are watching. I worry that he's doomed to nightmares for weeks, which is a terrible experience, especially if they're about sea monsters nipping at your toes when you're a helpless baby resting on a rock in the Aegean Sea. That's the one I usually get.

Skelly bangs a foot on the ground. He laughs wickedly, like he can't get enough of it. His teeth show, and that's unattractive. These days, he always laughs that ugly way. It used to be he felt bad about scaring people. It was during the last few years he started changing. First, he began to giggle. Now he lets go with a big, crazy sounding laugh that's so eerie I asked him about it last spring.

"Never noticed I been laughing," he said back then, a hand in a dirty pants pocket, the other gripping a beer. He raised his eyebrows like a detective.

"I noticed."

He seemed not to like what I was telling him, but he didn't appear surprised by the news, either. In thought, he lowered his chin to his chest, lost his drunken balance, and thumped his head against the side of his trailer, causing him to drop to his knees, where he turned over and sat in the leafy dirt. Winking at me, he took a few long gulps from the bottle and said, "I don't take pleasure in their fear, if that's what you're worried about, deary." He rested his sallow temple, like skin stained by egg yolk, against the tin siding. "I really don't take pleasure in their discomfort, love."

"I already know that you're not like that," I told him, because I didn't want him to think I was judging his bad behavior. "As long as I can remember, you've never been mean."

He narrowed his brows till they formed sharp, diamond-shaped lines above his nose. "As long as ya can remember, that's the key," he rasped. His mouth rested flatly, like the time Horst, the strong man, slugged him in his teeth, swelling his lips to resemble two gray, uncooked schnitzels. "Oh, child, if only I weren't ever mean or didn't ever do nothing dark and dreadful wrong. But I did. I… I been mean to folks. I done bad of the sort a bloke can't never live down. And I fear that one day you'll know me dirt and you'll see me different."

I hated when he acted as if he possessed terrible secrets of the sort you get in huge classical dramas with people wearing togas,

Ceasars (which were like Roman dictators), betrayals, and women who want to stab their chests for loving the wrong man. If Skelly actually had a secret he could never tell, he was smart enough to know not to say anything about it.

I remember how I searched off into the heavy darkness of the forest, which, as usual, seemed dangerous, like it was filled with evil fairytale dwarfs setting steel spring traps for humans. I was sure that if I stepped beyond those first few rough tree trunks, I'd never return back to my silver trailer.

I pivoted about and peered at Skelly, the man who was like a father to me. He drank too much in order to, he said, "disremember terrible things" or "celebrate good things." But if you think about that, disremembering terrible things is the exact opposite of celebrating good things, while everything between the two is partly one way or the other, giving him a constant excuse to drink.

Atop my head, I could feel my hair moving and reaching like it sought something to rip to shreds. It likes to rip things to shreds. "Did… did the bad things you say you did happen back when you were in Ireland?"

Skelly sucked at his front teeth before puckering his lips and letting them go. "No, not so much," he said softly. "I didn't do nothing back then that wasn't justifiable. In them days, we was trying to get the British off our bleeding land, so we did what we thought we had to. Never went out to hurt a man. If anything, my sin was the sin of silence, which is partway my sin now."

"Skelly, you don't have the sin of silence anymore."

He seemed confused.

"You're not silent when you laugh at upset guests."

He blinked and jammed his beer bottle into the grainy, brown dust, thought for a second, and pointed at me.

"What?" I asked.

His fingertip was trembling. "My sins are of a different sort of silence. The silence I mean is where a person hides useful, life-changing information from someone who can use it." He finished off his beer and whipped the empty bottle into the darkness of the forest, got up and staggered into his trailer. A moment later, he returned with a new one. Popping the top, pale foam roared out and onto his hands and grimy pants so that it looked like he'd wet himself. "So, you don't want me laughing no more?"

"Yeah. It seems ugly."

"Well, fine then I won't do it. Not even a speck."

Since, he's done a pretty good job of staying quiet, too.

2
THE RUNAWAY

When you live in a traveling carnival show, there are a lot of people who scare you, and some are actually the guests. In the Festival de Tordré, there's the creepy fortune teller, who can read your mind because your first thought when she's around is how you want to get away from her. Her eyes look like they could freeze you solid. Then there's the sword swallower, who, if you pass by her at the wrong time, seems like she's wrestling within herself not to take her sword and cut off your arm. Also the bearded lady constantly appears like she's lying to you, like she's just dropped a poison pill into your water so that she can get rid of you for good. And then there's Willem, who's part of the security team. I have a history with him, and I feel bad about it. However, he seems dangerous because he'd as soon drive over you in a car as pat your head. He's that way. But still, the very worst of all, is and will always be Rictus.

He thinks only about himself and no one else. His explosive anger gives me nightmares and makes my stomach queasy like I might barf. That's why, when I was eight years old and sure that I was capable of making a living wherever I wanted, I disregarded how he saved my life and tried to escape from the Festival de Tordré. That's how I learned that, unless I develop a really good plan, I should never run away again.

At the time, I'd been reading the Little Princess, which is a beautiful story about magical love between a father and his daughter. Because of it, I began to hope that maybe, in some small way, my parent's regretted what they'd done by putting me on the winged-foot rock. That feeling burned in me so brightly that I began to daydream about it in my cage. I envisioned myself paddling to the shores of a Greek island in the center of the Aegean Sea, walking past that foot-shaped rock and up to a familiar house. I wanted to show my parents that if I dressed in nicer clothes, like a cute dress, and washed my feet and hands so that they weren't so filthy, I was harmless and maybe even okay, especially if I wore a hat.

When I left my trailer to run away, it was so late that it was actually early. I started east and walked for hours. The moon fell and stars dimmed behind cloud cover that was like see-through curtain fabric. I didn't and don't like the darkness. I never have. It makes me scared of being bitten by something.

Cars passed. Their tiny engines sounded different from the American trucks and cars that the Festival de Tordré owned. Still, whenever I heard one coming, I jumped behind shrubs or hid at the edge of the woods that scared me so much. I worried that Rictus would come after me, not that he usually chased down employees who decided to leave his troupe. Instead, he simply kept the money he owed them, which was usually everything they'd earned. But my situation with him was different. He'd explained to me outright that I wasn't allowed to leave, that he was my guardian and I his dependant. He owned me.

That's why I was so cautious.

Above, the sky grew brighter in the east, so that I imaged it was midday in the communist European countries, where even in the summer the buildings and towns make you feel sad and unclean. When the Festival de Tordré toured behind the Iron Curtain, which is the name for the border between democratic and communist Europe, we'd learned that nobody over there had any money to spend on entertainment, a situation that so frustrated Rictus that he broke his foot kicking the rusty bumper on one of our hauling trucks.

Rictus.

As the sun brightened the sky, I trotted along wishing he had a broken foot once again. The first one had forced him to rest in bed for four weeks. He'd run the show by giving orders to Horst, the strong man, who passed them along to the rest of us like he was a military general. Still, while Rictus was recovering from his tender foot, rules got a lot looser

Ahead, the sun suddenly rose above a ridge. I could see its yellow behind a stand of pine trees that appeared to be drowning in melted butter. I smiled, felt surprisingly free, and started down toward a small German town.

Careful, I entered the first store I came to. Inside the stone building, it was tidy and clean so that the owners or their kids must have dusted it every day. I scanned the room, the dry goods, and various foods. It smelled like fresh baked bread and stinky cheese. I walked straight to the counter alongside a series of glass cases filled with meats. The nearest one sparkled and reflected the morning light as it beamed in through a window. "Sir," I said to the unhappy looking man behind the counter. "Sir, do you know which direction I need to travel to get to Mikonos?"

He frowned. "Mikonos?"

"Yes, sir."

"Vas ist, Mikanos?"

"Sir, I… I was told it's a small island off the coast of Greece in the Aegean Sea."

He replied in English, "Now how vould I know how to get you there?"

"I don't know."

"That's right, fräulein. I vould not know," he told me, leaning forward and looking down at me like I was tracking mud in his store.

Annoyed, I felt my hair nearly crackle like crossed electrical wires. "Thank you," I said, but he didn't respond. I hurried back out the door and up the street.

I passed ancient homes, some of them still scarred by gunfire and explosions from World War II. I thought about the man in the store and wondered if he'd lived back then. Maybe that was why he was such an unfriendly sort. Up the roadway, past a series of shops that weren't open yet, I spotted a large old lady walking a cat. I smiled and rushed forward toward her. "Ma'am," I called, "I am searching for the direction of Mikonos, an island."

She didn't reply.

"Ma'am, excuse me. Do you speak English?"

She stopped. "Da," she said, meaning she did.

"I'm searching for the direction of Mikonos, an Island. Have you ever heard of it?"

She stared, causing me to wonder if she was stupid.

I explained, "It's off the coast of Greece, in the Aegean Sea."

The woman tilted back and pointed at me. "Vait a minute, I know you."

I didn't reply.

"Da, of course I do."

"Nein," I told her calmly. That's means "no" in German.

"You're the monster child from that traveling show."

I stood still for a moment, shocked. I hardly recognized myself when I was made up to look like Medusa's Daughter, so how had she been able to figure out who I was? I wondered if she was some kind of witch with magic eyes that removed disguises.

Then someone shouted, "Maia!" and I forgot about the lady and her x-ray vision. I spun about and spotted Horst not a stones throw away.

Grinning cruelly, he climbed from the passenger side of his beaten up truck like a bear stepping out of a shipping crate.

"Oh, God!" Like a nest of weasels, my hair raised and hissed at him. I took off running as fast as I could go, up the pavement, across cobblestones, and past a stable. Behind me, I could hear Horst chasing me, his uneven breathing and his work boots striking the bumpy stone.

I glanced back and saw him bowl over the lady I'd been speaking to, causing her to crumble to the bumpy roadway and for her cat to flee.

I charged into a grassy field and slung myself through the rails of a fence. I stumbled along, trying not to sprain an ankle, and passed poorly kept goats and thousands of wildflowers before I realized that there was a roadway running along beside me. Over my shoulder, I heard a grinding of gears as a familiar truck zoomed up.

Once more, I switched directions, entering a line of trees, except I was running so fast I nearly took my head off on a low hanging branch that drummed the top of my skull with the sound of a spoon hitting the bottom of a cooking pot. I skidded to my knees before rising and jogging forward. Dark birds burst up around me, squawking and fluttering so that I worried I'd actually knocked myself out and was dreaming.

That's when I wished that Skelly had come with me even though I hadn't invited him. He might, if he wasn't too drunken, stand up for me. It made me sad that no one else would, that no one cared enough to chase Horst away, not even a brave stranger I could maybe fall in love with for being courageous like someone from the Boy's King Arthur book.

I leaped over a ditch and started sprinting up a small hill, except big tree roots caught the toes of my shoes and I pitched forward, landing on my stomach and knocking the wind out of me.

Wiping dirt from my tongue with the back of a hand, I rose, stopping when I saw Horst, only a few feet away, wearing the mean look I bet he wore back when he was one of Hitler's Nazi Youths, the teenage boys who were trained to hate Jews and Gypsies so that they could continue the Nazi empire for a thousand years. Too bad for Horst the Nazi empire went down in bullets and bombs.

Horst walked slowly toward me, his pudgy hands, the span of dinner plates, gripping and ungripping the air. "Please," I begged, terrified of what he might do. "I just wanted to go home. I… I just wanted to see my parents… again, okay, Mr. Horst? That's not a crime."

"Your parents! You do not have any parents, freak. Did not Rictus tell you they ver killed for being so hideous?" Squatting, he pushed me hard against the uneven ground, and my trembling arms collapsed under his strongman strength.

"Sorry," I cried. "I'm so sorry."

"Run-about, did Rictus say you could leave? Did Rictus give his permission?"

"No… sir. I… forgot to ask."

"Louder!" he screamed at me.

"No, sir!" In the distance I heard car doors thud shut. A few minutes slipped by. Behind me, people approached through dry leaves, kicking pebbles and twigs as they came. Without looking, I knew it was Atel and Willem, Horst's favorite assistants.

Bawling like a baby, I clawed at the dirt. I felt empty. I wasn't a daughter. I wasn't a friend. I was nothing, nothing, nothing.

"Hey," Horst said. "Hey quit!" he repeated in a suddenly urgent voice. "Little brat, let go!" I felt a distant tug at my scalp. "You're crushing my hand! You are crushing my wrist, bandersnatch."

Puzzled, I lifted my eyes to find Horst's glassy pupils large and spinning with panic. Where I had been too frightened to fight back, whatever separate intelligence controlled my living hair hadn't experienced a similar problem. I was only eight. My grip was weak, my hands tiny, and my legs short, but I suddenly recognized my strength, my ability to turn Horst's huge hand, which was purple, into a sagging mitten of powder and shards. Consciously, then, I tightened my hold so that something big inside his wrist snapped.

"Ah!" Horst hollered, his mouth open so wide that it looked as if he was about to bite into an enormous sandwich.

Feeling stronger, I rose to my knees and, as if in a trance, I directed a tentacle for his throat.

Then it was over. Something flashed past my forehead and struck my cheek so that pain vibrated through my skull. I flopped backward and scrounged, blinking and snorting in pain amongst leaves and underbrush. Rotating my achy gaze, I spotted Atel holding a rifle so that I knew he'd hit me with the hard back of it. Weighing it in his hands, he grinned at me. Beside him, stupid Willem laughed at my confusion while Horst rose to his feet and delicately supported his limp, massive hand like it was something precious and fragile he didn't want to drop. Slowly, slowly, the scene started to shift and blur and I was overcome with darkness, nothing but darkness. I was glad to escape them.

I woke long before we pulled onto the sideshow grounds, mostly because Atel, who was driving, got lost, causing the three of them to get in a long comical argument.

With my head placed against the metal dash, bumping painfully, I squinted downward and saw scraps of leaves, twigs, and dried dirt by my feet. It took me a second to recognize the floor of the truck we were driving in. My focus slowly sharpened, and I noticed the strangest thing. Two wavy wires were tying Atel's bootlaces to the steel frame of the truck seat. It was really odd. Dizzy, I watched them work for a few minutes till, with a jolt, I realized that the wires weren't wires but two cord-thin locks of my hair, at which point I slammed closed my eyes. I didn't want anything to do with it.

In camp, Atel parked the car behind Rictus' tent. "Finally," he said. "Was harder finding our way back than catching this fly?"

"What fly?" Willem wanted to know because he's not smart.

"This one. Medusa's Daughter?" Atel tapped me like I was still unconscious.

Very seriously, Willem replied, "She's not a fly. She's a girl."

Atel growled, "And you're a brainless…"

Horst cut him off. "Can you see that I need a doctor? Can you see, I need help? Could you hurry up?"

Annoyed, Atel opened his door and leaped from the truck, except he suddenly pin-wheeled his arms and lunged forward off balance, his narrow hands grappling to hold onto the truck window. "Horst, can you help, my bloody bootlaces are stuck on something?"

"My arm is broken!"

Atel's fingers screeched down the glass till he got to the metal window frame, where he slipped and fell, shoulder first, into one of the hundreds of mud puddles surrounding our camp. "Damn it!" he hollered, spluttering in the water till Willem came around and cut his boots free with a knife.

Rising, Atel yanked me from the car and held me by an elbow. "Did you do that to me?"

I played like my knees wouldn't even lock.

"Did you!?"

"Atel," Horst blurted, "she can't even stand. Do you think she can tie knots?"

Willem grabbed me by my waist and flopped me over his shoulder. Then, robotically, he carried me around to Rictus' living quarters, where he dumped me on the dirt floor.

I opened my eyes and Rictus glowered down at me.

Behind me, Horst howled, "Hey, boss. Boss! We got her. But look! Look at my arm. She crushed the bones."

Rictus grinned, slamming the point of his walking stick into the dirt. "And you call yourself a strongman! You let an eight-year-old outmuscle you. Pathetic, Horst!" Horst seemed embarrassed, and I was glad.

Bending down, Rictus snagged me by a belt loop and plopped me roughly on a stool, where I sat woozy, envisioning myself like a melting piece of modeling clay.

"Why?" he asked me. "Why? Did I not furnish you with everything you've ever needed, a beautiful trailer, a shining career, and food to fill your belly? Have I not cared for you with purpose and concern?"

I nodded. "But... I don't want to be a freak."

"Well you are."

"And I'm... scared people here, sir, and of... you some. And... and I hate to be scared and live scared. I hate it."

"As you should," he said, and started circling me slowly. "But you will and should always be frightened. You're a freak. The general populace would kill you in an instant. Therefore, I control your existence. I keep you safe from a world that would despise you. I keep you all safe. Do you think you're the only freak here who fears me? Do you?"

"No."

"Say it with force."

"No!"

He began circling faster, stopped and snared my chin so that I looked him in his cold eyes. "You little brat. You run again, and I'll haul you back here a lot worse for the wear. I will punish you till you cower and beg to stay. I'll turn you into the animal that you are."

My cheek started to throb again, and I started to cry. I couldn't help it. I never wanted to feel vulnerable in front of Rictus, but I always did. "Yes… sir. I… understand."

He snorted and spat out a huge gob of spit, which caused my stomach to churn. Then he pointed toward the tent exit, his multicolored suit coat shimmering in the daylight. "Now, outside with you. Go face the others, whose well-being your selfishness put into jeopardy. Go face the ones who struggle to make you comfortable and ask in return that you simply do as you are told."

Like a puppet, a prisoner, or both, I slipped off the stool and staggered toward the tent flap. I pushed it open and found that nearly all of the sideshow's workers, from freaks to carnies were situated in two parallel lines, forming a long pathway between them.

I looked back at Rictus, who grabbed me by my collar and held me in place. I begged, "I'm sorry! I won't do it again, sir."

He grinned. "You're not as sorry as you're going to be, Medusa's Daughter." Everyone laughed at that, and he raised his square-fingered hands like he was shushing a church crowd. "She told me," he called, "she thinks herself better than all of you. She thinks she would be properly suited to life with others less ghastly. Show her what we think of her arrogance. Let her bathe in it!"

They cheered for a moment. Rictus shushed them again, cleared his throat, and spit right on me. It was foul. Worse, he took a foot and pushed my hip so that I stumbled part way down the path.

That's when it started. People aimed their lips at me like they were the barrels of guns. I felt like a mechanical duck in a shooting arcade. I could feel my clothes begin to soak through. I could feel my heart breaking from sadness and disgust. I wanted to collapse, but my hair, as always, wanted to fight back. And that scared me so that I stayed in the center of the corridor between everyone for fear that my angry coils would ravel around arms or shoulders and snap them like toothpicks.

Closing my eyes, I started running till I collided into someone. Immediately, I smelled the sour odor of alcohol rising from unwashed skin, and I knew it was Skelly without even looking.

Like a fallen angel, Skelly pulled back the different sides of his stale sports coat jacket and enfolded me gently. Safe like that, I choked then cried loudly, gurgling in the deepest, darkest sadness. I didn't even know why. It didn't make sense to blubber when it was all over. But I was ten, and, I guess, with my wet face buried that way, it seemed like I didn't have any hope or purpose or possibility. None in the world. I was trapped in the Festival de Tordré till the day Rictus croaked, which I hoped would be soon.

3

GUARDIAN ANGEL.

After that, I haven't cared for most of the people I live with. I didn't trust them. I knew they watched out for themselves and nobody else. They reminded me of sharks that eat their shark babies. I could tell, if they got hungry, they'd start eating each other. Nothing came first for them but themselves. Nothing, that is, but Rictus, and he came first out of fear.

That night, after getting spit on, I sat in Skelly's trailer with an empty, aching stomach. I looked down at the grungy little flower-patterned couch beneath me while he set about cleaning my face with a partly dirty dish cloth that smelled like dog's breath. But he meant well. Plus, a dog's breath dish cloth is better than any type of human spit. It's just the law. That's why people let dogs lick them but don't want to be licked by other people.

Skelly got me a cup of tea, and I put it on my trembling knees. Around my feet, decorating most every surface in his little living area were dozens of empty liquor bottles, some dusty as a haunted house living room, others new and turned over, like they'd been kicked or dropped and never picked up.

"Maia," he finally said, "what pains me is that I could've helped ya. My god, lassy, ya should've told me what ya was gonna do, and I would've helped. For the life of me, I would've seen ya gone from here."

I was so weakened, I couldn't even answer back.

"Oh, lassy, we need to get ya out of here. Without a doubt. But we needs to do so in such a ways as to prevent Rictus from finding ya ever again. Do ya see?"

He picked up a bottle that was on its side, studied it, and took a sip. "If ya weren't his best freak, he would make an example of ya, he would. Then where would that leave me?"

I don't know so I don't answer.

"Lost, Maia. I'd be lost. I am here to watch out for ya. That is the only reason I'm still here." He leaned forward and squeezed one of my hands. He studied my face like a father whose been soaked in liquor the way German pickles are in barrels. Close up, I could see how his eyes were bloodshot, the skin beginning to sag on both sides of his nose and on the far side of his lids. I wasn't sure of his age, but I didn't think he was considered old for an adult. Even then, I knew it probably wasn't the years that made him appear like he did, it was how he'd lived them. He said, "I fear... now, you've set course in dangerous waters."

"I... I only wanted to see my parents again."

"Rictus says they're dead."

"But he's a liar. I've heard him lie about a million times."

"Dear, even if they are alive, do ya really want to see them again? I mean, they left ya to die."

"That's what he says. But even if it's true, maybe now I'm not as bad as they might think. Do you know?"

He shook his head and stared upward at the roof of his trailer. "You'll break me heart one day. Yes, lassy, of course you're not so bad. You're not awful at all. Not in the least… and ya should know ya never were. Not one day in your life have ya been awful."

"Except for when I was born."

He stared at me. "As you said, Rictus is a liar."

"Except I think that story's real." I moved my hair around to make a point.

"You're harmless, child. Harmless."

"How about injuring Willem?"

He stared at me and stood, groaning as he rose. "Unfortunately, we got to cut this short cause I got to take ya back to Rictus. I hate it, but I do. I'm so sorry. I'm sorry, dear."

I looked up at him, shocked. "He's going to punish me. Do you know?"

"I know, little love, and I can't do nothing. If I try to stop him, it'll be worse for ya. I know how he operates."

I was devastated that Skelly would surrender me that way. It left a deep hole inside my chest. "Please, don't," I begged.

"I'll make sure it ain't so terrible, love."

But he couldn't. I was locked in a box truck for a week. I was only allowed to leave to do my show.

I'm seated on my bed, awake from a familiar and consistent nightmare. I have the same one three nights out of a week. In it, I'm floating on a raft. That's strange because I've never been on a raft, not once in my life. Over the raft, the sun is bright and the sky is blue. Desperately, I grab for something that has slipped beneath the choppy water. My living hair is dipping and rising in and out like safety lines. I peer down, but it's dirty and I can't see very deep. Momentarily, I'm gripped by an overwhelming feeling of loss. Someone important has just drown. And since

Skelly is the only important person in my life, I decide it's him, that he has died.

After the dream, I always wake up sweating and breathing hard. To calm down, I stretch my legs, which can feel cramped because I sleep in a tight ball that a bear could roll around with his paw, not that there are any bears in my trailer.

After a while, I go to a cupboard and find some bread and a piece of cheese for breakfast, then I sit and read an old magazine called National Geographic I found on a table in the food tent so long ago I can't even remember. Every few months, I reread it because it's like traveling the world.

Time goes by. I get to an article on crocodiles in Australia, then a dull one on a song bird in America, followed by one more on African men who jump from high towers and fall till they're suddenly saved by vines tied to their ankles. Rictus doesn't say I am, but I consider myself human, and because of that I think that I'm not the only human who does ridiculous things to themselves. To me, diving from high towers is even worse than dressing up like a monster. A lot worse. And I don't dress that way because I want to. I have to.

I lift the magazine up and look at the men's faces just as the vines pull tight. Their eyes are gigantic and pained. Each has their mouth wide open, their bad teeth showing. I bet they're ankles feel as if they might tear off.

Who does that sort of thing?

For some reason, I start to feel better about myself.

I'm not on a raft and I'm not diving off a tower with my ankles roped to a vine.

I get dressed and go for a walk through the German countryside, which is different from the Spanish countryside. That's where The Festival de Tordré was touring over the winter, before we drove up here to Germany for the summer. Those places felt dry and bright, the sun warm. It's darker and heavier here. The trees feel similar to slippery castle towers. The rocks in the ground feel hard and unfriendly, as if they are the large remains of cruel and extinct dragons. I might have read too many Grimm's Fairytales when I was younger, but German forests are spooky. Walking through them can cause my shoulders to shiver unexpectedly, like icy cold witches keep staring at the spine of my back.

I decide to think of Australia, which is a country from the National Geographic magazine I just read. If I was there, I'd have to be careful about wandering near a giant, saltwater crocodile, the type that eats people like snacks. If I was in Canada, which I know about from other things I've read, I'd have to worry about bears, both grizzly and polar. And if I happened to visit India, I might step on a king cobra snake that's got a deadly, venomous bite. I know that because of the story Rikki-Tikki-Tavi, my almost favorite book of all time that's about a mongoose, a nice boy, and two murderous king cobra's whose names I forget. Anyway, it seems like everywhere is a little dangerous except Germany, which feels dangerous. It's weird.

I return a couple of hours later, sit and read the rest of Pygmalion, which is a play by a guy named George Bernard Shaw, who seems like a stuffy boring man. Still, the story is good. Whenever I read it, I wonder if I might one day experience something as wonderful as Eliza Doolittle, the star. Like her, I want to get plucked from my current existence and get placed in high society. How great would that be, to be a beautiful lady after never feeling that way before in your life?

I rise, turn, and check myself in my mirror. I could be pretty—maybe. I could be if I had good clothes and could wash and make up my face. But Rictus doesn't want me to feel like a human girl.

I study my cheeks in the mirror. I tilt my head and curl my hair about my neck like it's a little animal getting comfortable.

One piece rises up and softly touches my chin. I drape my eyes half shut, which is what starlets do, and I pucker my lips the way I've seen on movie posters, especially the French ones. "Bonjour, mademoiselle," I say to myself in French. In English, that means, "Hello, young lady."

Since I don't know any more French, I tell me, "You're very pretty, Miss."

I nod and touch my fingers to my left collar bone like I'm shy but also flattered by my comment. "Do you think I'm just a little beautiful?" I ask.

But before I can answer, the door to my trailer whips open, and Rictus barrels in.

"Rictus, you should knock," I blurt, stepping away from the mirror and hoping he hasn't heard me.

"And you should be careful about who you're talking to." He tucks back some of his straight hair, hair that appears ironed flat due to never getting washed.

"Get dressed in your rags, Maia. Put your stage makeup on. We've got an ink-stained wretch from The Berlin Times or Stars and Stripes, one of those sorry rags. He wants a few snap shots of you for his paper, so... be good. We're trying to sell tickets."

I nod nervously, wishing I hadn't said that he should knock. When Rictus threatens someone, he's never shy about progressing from a threat to action or from action then a threat. What I mean is, once, I saw him take his walking stick and hit an auto mechanic who was working on one of our trucks. The guy fell out dazed on the floor, and then Rictus threatened him by saying, "Now you stop fiddling with that wire, or I'll give you a headache." But he'd already given him a headache, so what was the use in saying it.

"Hurry up," Rictus snaps at me, his jowls shaking. He leaves, stops and says, "The man wants to see a freak, and you better give it to him, Medusa's Daughter."

"I will," I promise. My hair reaches over and pulls the trailer door closed. I shake my head and peer into the mirror. "Quit thinking, mademoiselle," I tell myself. "Don't ruin a good day. Just stop." I breathe deep. "It's a good day. It's a good day," I say, trying to convince myself.

I leave my trailer and walk through the empty sideshow grounds, eventually arriving behind the midway, sliding under the tent, and climbing into the back of my cage. Shortly, the photographer guy arrives with Rictus. He grins and whispers at me, "Now aren't you an exotic young woman."

The way he talks, I can tell he thinks that the dirt under my fingernails and the grime up and down my arms is attractive. I'd bet he even likes my fangs and dark glasses, which really don't look good on me at all. I can't help but wonder about the kind of person who thinks that Medusa's Daughter is attractive. After about an hour behind the camera, he walks over to Rictus and says, "Under different circumstances, she might be alluring, yes?"

Rictus levels his gaze on me. "Under different ones, you might be right."

When the photographer is reloading his camera with film, I send a lock of hair through the fencing, pick up a small stone, and toss it at him, bouncing it off his gray temple from about twenty feet.

Wincing, the guy looks around, confused.

Another few hours go by, and Rictus and the man decide to share a bottle of wine outside my cage. I recognize that Rictus is trying to make me uncomfortable. He wants me to stay locked in my cage because he's still mad that I told him to knock on my trailer door.

Irritated, I sit down and pull my knees up against my chest. I lean back against splintery planks and try to rest, except I'm cold and can't get warm. The burlap sack I wear is a thick weave, if that's what you call it, that allows the wind through. Due to its unattractiveness, you won't ever find it in a fashion magazine.

Closing my eyes, I listen to the two men talk about their days in America, recount stories about their arrival in Europe.

"Been here ever since," the cameraman says. But his life has been boring.

"When I first arrived," Rictus says, "I was running from the law. Running. And I had this crummy little Festival de Tordré I'd won in a bet in Indianapolis and nothing else. Fact is, we were bleeding money till me and this fella I met formed a relationship. He had ideas about how to jumpstart the money situation. Right off, he triples the number of pickpockets and insists on getting us better attractions that families might want to see. Then we enter into the gambling business, which is like printing money. Bad thing is, soon enough, I owe him half the show."

"So I make plans on how to get my share back. He's a slimy pigeon, but I'm dangerous, see. You don't put slimy against dangerous. Slimy will lose. So, this guy struts around the grounds like he's important, and I let him act that way. Why not? Money's flowing. Time goes by, and we go to fetch that beast," and I knew he was talking about me, "and I kill two birds with one stone. I got back the other half of my business, and every American GI in every free country on this continent comes to see Medusa's Daughter wiggle her bangs. It's sad." To emphasize his statement, Rictus lifts his wine glass and drinks.

The newspaper photographer leans forward. "So, whatever happened to that partner, eh, Mr. Fitch?"

"Oh, he's still around. Didn't take long before I got him so beat down he doesn't know whether he's coming or going. Nope, he never knew what I had in store for him. All it took was applying a few screws to the proper locations, and he broke. It's what I'm good at, breaking people. It's a gift."

I breathe deep and fold my arms across me. I'd never known that Rictus had once had a partner in The Festival de Tordré or that the man, whoever it was, was still around.

The early afternoon shifts to late afternoon, and the first visitors eventually arrive, meaning I'll be stuck in my cage till nearly midnight. Hours pass. I grow more and more uncomfortable. My hips ache and my back gets tight. I wrap my hair to the top of the cage and it lifts me softly off the floor so that my hips feel better. That's how I hang, like a right-side-up bat. Late in the night, Rictus stops by. "Hello my little monster," he says, chewing on a cigar. "What do you think now? Do you agree that I can enter your trailer whenever I like, mouse?"

I don't nod, because I'd have to break out of character, in order to do it. I just stare.

"Good," he tells me. "Good. I believe we've worked this out sufficiently."

When the last drunken visitor is escorted out of the sideshow by Horst and Atel, I crawl from my cage. My feet are raw and my skin is red from wearing sack cloth for so long.

I walk back toward my trailer. Around me, I hear the entire Festival closing down for the night. I circle around and behind the midway so that I don't have to see anyone.

Sadly, I spot Horst walking back from his trailer. He's still in costume, strutting like an overstuffed, plucked turkey with skinny legs and a cigar in its beak. I despise him with nearly every bone in my body. Staring at the ground, I try to walk right past, but he doesn't let me go. He never does.

"Vell, look who it is. Rictus' kitten."

"I might be his kitten, but at least I'm not his monkey."

He considers what I've said before smashing one hand into the palm of another. "Who are you saying is a monkey, Maia?"

"Let's see, you drag your knuckles when you walk and have a face like an orangutan's rear."

"I don't drag my knuckles," he replies.

"My mistake."

He points at me with a cigar. "And, vhat's the rear of an orangutan?"

"It's the butt of a monkey." I turn and head for my trailer.

Behind me, Horst absorbs what I've said for a moment, then he hollers, "You don't talk to me this vay, runabout! You don't."

For some reason, I stop and turn around. "I just did," I tell him, and my voice sounds unnatural, like a hiss. When I was younger, I was terrified of Horst. But as I've gotten older, I've noticed something about him. Without permission from Rictus, he would soil his pants instead of go to the bathroom. He's a poodle. He's a little baby. Sometimes, when he stands beside Rictus, he even trembles like a miniature dog from Mexico who wants to be stroked.

I have a strange desire to pick a fight with him, and I've never in my whole life picked a fight with anyone. I can feel my hair shift its full, angry attention in Horst's direction. Then, once more I turn and walk away, trying, as I go, to feel less dangerous.

In the darkness, I pass into the woods, where I stop to breathe before I reach my trailer. I don't want to go into my room feeling like an elephant shut in a shoebox.

I close my eyes, and pieces of bark fall down on my head as hundreds of strands of hair begin to pick the trunk of a tree smooth like piranha fish attacking a cow leg. I've never understood why my hair does that sort of thing. Pulling away, I watch it continue to strip the tree till it's out of reach, then it settles on my head like it's suddenly tired and calm. I turn and walk down the path to my silver trailer, where I find Skelly leaning against the front door and guzzling back some type of liquor.

"Hello, me lassy."

I smile sadly. "Skelly?"

"Yes, gal?"

"Are you a mess already?

"Yup."

"You're always a mess these days."

"You're right, deary. It's for the reason that this place is a madhouse. It drives me to the bottle."

"Anything drives you to the bottle?"

"Seems that way, don't it. But my drinking's all circumstantial."

"What's that mean, Skelly?"

"Means," he says, and sways dramatically, "if I'd never left home, I'd have never touched the drink, and I'd have meself a respectable job working in some Belfast factory. I'd be gently smashing Irish granite into pebbles or something."

"Skelly, I'm not trying to be mean, but you should go home, then, and save yourself. I worry about you. I worry you're going to drink so much you'll die. People can, you know? I read about it."

"Everyone's gonna die, Maia. Besides, go home to what? Civil War? Unemployment? To what, me love? I got an important position here. I ain't just a regular shill. I'm a guardian angel watching over an innocent child so she don't get hurt by none of the sluggards she works with."

I smile. I've always enjoyed the way he talks. "You don't look like an angel."

"It's cause I got me wings shot off 'bout twelve years ago when I selected me a business partner. They don't grow back, ya see."

I don't reply.

"Well if you're gonna sit there all quiet like in front of my trailer, least tell me a story about this town and its residents, especially since we're leaving in the morning, and I ain't even given it a glance, yet.

"For your information, this is my trailer," I tell him.

"Course it is. Now, about that story?"

"I haven't been to town, either."

"God, you're a bore."

"No, I'm not," I say, smiling.

"Then tell me something, girl."

"Well, earlier today, a kid tried to spit on me."

"And what did ya do about it?"

"Nothing. I just moved out of the way."

"Should've tied him in a knot, or plucked out his hair one piece at a time."

I directed my thoughts away from the incident. "I just want to forget it."

Skelly took some long gulps from his bottle and wiped his mouth with a wrist. "I'm telling ya, ya should've gone after the twit, Maia."

I appreciate how he's trying to be funny, but I don't feel silly. I lean forward and talk to him like I have an awful secret. "I couldn't. You know how it's been. I've been losing my mind with anger. You saw it a few times. I tried to attack that man who poked me with that coat hanger last week. I... I've decided I can't let myself get mad, or I'll become the monster I pretend I am."

He laughs at me. "Nah ya won't, Maia. Ya ain't no beast or ancestor of one. And don't go forgetting that neither. Anything else interesting occur?"

I think through my day, stuck in my cage like I was. I'm glad to be off the subject of anger. "This morning, I saw a lady get out a long black car and go visit Rictus. I think she was the mayor. She was dressed beautiful, too, and had a bodyguard or something. Can you imagine being dressed that way?"

"Nope, don't got a notion in me head."

"Nice, I bet, is how she felt."

Skelly finished off the bottle and pointed at me with the neck. "Bet she was getting paid off by Rictus. Bet he was paying off the mayor so that he could get away with running a gambling racket while we were here. We used to do it all the time. That was my idea." He smiles.

I love Skelly deeply, but, sometimes, he says things that don't make sense. I attribute that to his drinking. More than a dozen times, I've watched him drink himself into a stupor that took him days to bounce back from. I worry that his poor heart will one day stop beating due to what he's done.

Watching me, Skelly wobbles and lurches backwards, where he bangs against the side of my trailer. Lifting a hand and pointing at me, he says, "Lassy, had me an exchange with the fat lady today on account of me innocently crunching that cow hoof she calls a foot. Well let me tell you something in case you've forgotten, she's got the personality of a Pamplona bull. Ain't nothing feminine 'bout her. Nothing."

I laugh. He's never had anything nice to say about the fat lady, who's incredibly unfriendly. I grin at him, look away, then look back. I want to ask him a question. "Skelly," I begin, "you think it's weird how everyone's always unfriendly around here?"

He shrugs, pulls a silver flask from his back pocket and tips the contents down his skinny throat. "I don't think it is. In actual fact, sweetheart, I don't think it's strange at all. To me, being deceitful and angry seems like a natural human state. That's my angle on it, dear. Take my homeland for example…"

"Okay," I tell him.

"We're all born and raised on the same hard luck island of Ireland. We've all been spit on and kicked round for centuries. Folks call us the pigeons of Europe, and it don't matter if you're successful or poor, protestant or catholic."

I like pigeons and ask, "What's so bad about being a pigeon?"

"Ya know what a pigeon is, Maia?"

"It's a bird."

"For sure a bird. But more than that, it's a flyin' rat. It's a flyin' rat and nothing more. That's what everyone thinks of the Irish. Flyin' rats."

I'm not sure I believe him, but I don't say anything.

"So you would think, under those kind of bad conditions, we'd all feel like we're in the same sorry boat. You'd think we Irish would get along. But we don't for nothing. We all scrap for our little bit. On top of that, we go exploding bombs and killing fellow flying rats in the name of religion and the like, which ain't so very religious to me."

"Nope. It don't make sense. Just like this here mothy sideshow. We all get the short end of it from Rictus, and most of us have got his man Horst on our ass twice daily, but we don't come together a lick. We all wants our little bit of the little bit there is, and to hell with everyone else. It's just like Ireland. Same thing. It's the sad, sorry, screwed-up human condition."

I wait a moment before saying, "Skelly, there must be a reason the Irish don't get along."

"Oh, there is. Dear, it's cause we spent a good bit of time killing each other. You heard of the civil war in Northern Ireland?"

I'd heard of the Spanish Civil War but not any others except the one in America. "No."

"Well, suffice it to say there is and was one. It's the Catholics against the Protestants and Brits. Worse, since I'm a bloody Catholic from Belfast, which is in Northern Ireland, I grew up in the middle of it. I grew up in the slums of a crumbling city where whole portions of Catholic communities were gutted by the British army and partially flattened by Catholic terrorists. I hated it. Ya get real desperate in them situations, Maia. Ya do things ya shouldn't. I learned all there was to know about hate and backstabbing from my own neighbors and my ownself, don't ya know. So when I got old enough, I chose to leave it all behind, all the bombing, all the intimidation, and the name-calling, and I came here, to mainland Europe, to start over and wash my hands clean. I wanted to become a better person, but what did I do, I started the old Irish practice of backstabbing and hateful things. Guess it was in me heart and soul."

I don't like it when he talks that way. "You aren't hateful, Skelly, and you know that."

He runs a dirty hand through his hair. "Oh, love," he says, "ya don't know what I done, but I do, and it don't surprise me that folks can be so hateful to one another. All of us here in the festival, we're all one in the same, losers, scrapers, scrappers, and scum." He smiled. "Except for ya, Maia."

"You insult yourself too much," I tell him.

"Actually, I don't insult myself enough, girly. So, just to be mean, I'm gonna sit right here and drink till I drop. On the way, I'm gonna forget this bloody world, too. I'm gonna forget it and my sorry place in it."

That's what Skelly does, too. He guzzles more liquor, slumping and slumping till he rests on the ground like a curled up mutt. With a hand over his head, he asks for me to forgive him, which I get tired of and go inside my trailer, lock the door, and read *Animal Farm*, a book that Skelly loaned me, till late in the night. Meanwhile, Skelly crawls beneath my trailer and passes out. If there is one thing I have learned from him, it is that people should never, not once, take a sip of alcohol. It makes them sad and sorry for themselves. Also, it makes their breath bad enough to kill weeds and almost you.

In the morning, I check on him before going for a walk in the forest. He's still breathing, thank goodness, but he looks as if he's got the flu. His skin is clammy and pale, and his mouth is open so that a small yellow leaf has actually drifted down and into it without him even knowing, causing me to wonder if a person can choke to death on something as soft as a leaf. Delicately, I pick it out with a few strands of hair. When I do it, I have to hold my breath due to his.

Never drink, I tell myself. Never.

Hesitantly, I leave him, passing beneath tall, gloomy trees, my bare feet crunching tiny acorns and twigs settled atop the dirt path. My hair reaches out and lifts branches that stretch out and into my way. I hear birds and look upwards to find small ones making their way from one edge of the horizon to the other. The sky behind them is wonderful, so blue that calling it blue doesn't sound right. It's super blue, maybe.

For reasons I can't explain, I feel good, even in those German woods. So I suddenly run and jump a ditch with a little stream flowing slowly at the bottom of it. Stopping, I turn, lean, and study the eddying water, my toes pressing against the cool dirt. I can see my reflection, and I try, for no reason, to picture myself as a normal person. Then a few locks extend down and wrap around stones that they lift and place in my hands. Weighing them, I throw one at a tree, playing that it's Rictus, who I hit right in the teeth, knocking all of his front ones out. Then, I weigh the next stone and whip it so that I strike him in one of his squinty eyes. I laugh. "Did that hurt?" I ask, trying to sound funny. "Aww... does Rictus have a hurt eyeball?"

I keep going.

Because it's Germany, there are pockets of cool air along the trail, so I have to wrap my arms tightly around myself to stay warm. I don't mind. It's nice to have variety since my days are always so similar.

Something catches my eye, and I look sideways. I spot a fox walking exactly parallel to me over a thick, flat bed of pine needles and between tall, straight evergreens.

I kneel and hold out a hand. The fox stops. Wild animals have never been afraid of me, whereas the tame pets from people's homes or laps scatter when I'm around.

The fox's tail is a dirty but brilliant copper color. It sizes me up before approaching. Its legs are narrow and fragile looking, about the thickness of an adult man's thumb but much longer.

Seeing them makes me worried for the animal, as if the poor thing is too delicate to survive in the wild. It also has a sweet, narrow face that doesn't appear capable of saving itself much less chasing down a rodent.

It doesn't growl when my fingers move from its muzzle to its small head and pointy ears. I rub its dusty fur back and it sits. I smile at it. When I stand, it rises and places its front paws up on my thigh like it wants to dance. "You're beautiful but dirty," I tell it.

It whines.

I say, "Guess what, mister, I'm sorry, but I've got to go. I can't stay or someone will wonder where I went. They'll think I'm trying to run away, and wouldn't that hurt?"

Back at the Festival grounds, it's moving day, and people are everywhere, yanking out poles and steaks, curling ropes and rolling colorful tent canvas. I don't mind moving days. People leave me alone because they're so busy. I've always realized that if I intended on escaping The Festival de Tordré again, moving day would be a good time.

I yawn.

Today, I'm so tired I wouldn't get far. I was up late reading *Animal Farm*. In it, a pig named Napoleon rules other farm animals by spreading lies and using attack dogs to scare everyone into obedience. Napoleon tells everyone around him that he means well, that he's nice, but the truth is he only thinks of himself and no one else. For an animal story, it was good. It reminded me of the way Rictus runs the festival.

In time, I head back to my camper. Skelly is gone. I go look for him but everyone is so busy I don't have any luck. I come back and put my folding chair on top of my couch and pick up a few of Skelly's beer bottles. I don't like for him to litter. It's like wounding the earth.

Shortly, Atel and Willem, come looking for me, and, without saying a word, they crunch their hands about my elbows, squeezing too hard. Then, together they pull me right over to my trailer. My hair hisses the entire time, like king cobras from the book Rikki-Tikki-Tavi, which I already said is one of my almost favorites because of the cute, brave mongoose whose name is Rikki-Tikki-Tavi.

"Bratling," Atel says to me. "Tramp. Runabout. If you're not going to help, then you should make a point of staying out of our way while we pack your festival."

My hair crouches like it might launch at them as they shove me into my trailer and lock the door from the outside. I hate Atel and Willem. I hate them both. Breathing hard, I sit, appalled by my thoughts of revenge.

4
SEE THE
BEASTY

Forests and towns slide past. When I'm tired, they blur, like thick impressionist paint instantly covering the details of a photograph. Over the roadways, my trailer rocks up and down, so that I can imagine I'm on an ocean and slowly sailing for shore in a strange capsule, like a submarine that can't be driven or steered.

When I'm not so tired, I look out the windows to see stone castles and grand cathedrals that soar upward like pictures I saw of the Apollo rocket ships the Americans shot into space.

It's funny—or not—but I know that the people who built the castles and cathedrals of Europe died of the plague or a thousand other illnesses, but I can't help thinking that the old days must've been magical. I can't help wanting to live back then. I see huge fields dotted with cows and sheep, and I imagine jousting matches and sword fighting competitions. I see little towns and I think of soup and crusty bread served by women wearing aprons. Whereas the age and feel of German forests seems somehow evil, German villages are like toy landscapes. They look made of tiny dollhouse parts.

I see the lovely sun burn quietly above the trees before shivering against the horizon. In the distance, mountains glow as if sprinkled with golden flecks. Where the sun appears to sink into the far off fields, I imagine that it is turning into a liquid and that gold is filling lakes and streams. I want to swim in them and turn my skin into a beautiful, bronze tone. I want to be known for being shiny more than eerie.

It's night time when we pull into Wadern. I help Horst and his men set up my trailer so that they might quickly leave. I pull out my chair and put it out front. When everything is in place, Horst waits by my door.

I open it to get away from him, but he follows me inside and says. "If you need help fluffing your pillow, you tell Horst."

I ignore him, and wish I was someone else. He leaves and I keep wishing. I wish that for two more hours. I want to be one of those clean-scrubbed girls who comes to the show and wrinkles her nose when they see me in my cage. I want to swim in a golden stream.

I look for something to read and find a love story called *The Captain's Soul Mate.* It's awful. I found it on the bleachers by my cage one night and picked it up the same way I pick up all American books before the area is cleaned. But nearly every page makes my blood boil.

Finally, Skelly comes around. "Lassy?"

I unlock the door and hold the book in his face. "Is this story real? Do people in America really fall in love this way?"

He grins. He's had a bit to drink.

"Well, let's see what'cha got there. Oh, now look at this. The Captain's Soul Mate, eh? Well, be assured it's a bunch of garbage. But, yes, dear, people fall hopelessly and passionately in love all the time, not just in America neither."

I don't believe him. Nobody I've ever met, other than Skelly, seems capable of caring for anyone other than themselves. "I'm quitting. I hate this book. It makes me mad. It's fake that he cares for her the way he does. I mean, he saves her from pirates by attacking the entire ship with just a knife he holds in his teeth."

"Ah, that's love, ain't it?" Skelly jokes.

I hold it out. "The guy dives into a stormy ocean and rescues her as she's sinking slowly to the bottom."

"The man's driven by passion. What can I say?"

"He saves her from cannibals with a sword and a monkey he trains in about ten minutes."

Skelly points at me and smiles wonderfully, so that I smile too. "Ten minutes? A monkey? That's bad."

"That's what I mean."

"Throw that piece of tripe out!" he hollers.

Because I don't know, I ask, "What's tripe?"

"It's the stomach of a cow, me girl. Also, it means the book's garbage."

"The stomach of a cow," I repeat softly, visualizing the book as a cow gut. I look at him, grin, and say, "Yeah, it's tripe."

"Sure it is." He laughs. "Training a monkey in ten minutes… Please!"

At sunrise, my trailer, which is sitting out in the open, heats up so that I can hardly breathe. Rising, I put on a coat, long pants, and shoes, and I go outside for a breath of cool air. Within about a minute, I start to shiver and decide to head to the dining tent. Walking slowly, I feel my hair stretching outwards like a dangerous sea plant on an underwater reef. I hear voices ahead, but I don't hear Rictus, so I enter. And there he is.

He's arranging to send Horst, Atel, and the sword swallower to paste up Festival de Tordré posters around town. Horst frowns at me and says, "Eh, Rictus, ve should pull Medusa along chained in a vagon, no? It vould draw a crowd."

Rictus studies Horst as if he's pathetic. "Tell me, Horst," he says harshly, "why should I give those bloodsuckers something for free when I can charge them for a glimpse?"

Horst straightens. "It… it might drum up the extra good business is vhy."

Rictus' eyes narrow. They remind me of two tiny stars in a far off section of the sky. "How about you shutting that disgusting Kraut trap of yours, Horst, and leave the marketing to me!"

Horst's face drains of all color. He fumbles at the buckle of a bracer, which is basically a big leather wrist band that weightlifters wear. "Of course, Rictus," he says.

After breakfast, I go back to my silver trailer. Before going inside, I stop and look at it, shift my gaze and study the trunks of the trees I'm beneath. Through them, I can see the fields beyond. They seem to rush all of the way to the distant mountains that the sun rises over. No wonder I'd gotten so hot this morning.

I step around, and my hair grows in thickness, the individual locks spooling seamlessly outwards, as if there's a giant cylinder wench in my skull where a brain should be. Like a tremendous tarantula spider, coils swarm the metal trailer hitch like it's a meal, and as easy as can be, I move my trailer out of the way of the morning sun.

Done, my hair retreats, and I go inside. It's still hot, but I sit and think for a moment. The sideshow doesn't open for seven hours, so I take my hat and a few coins, put on my street clothes, including shoes, and leave to find Skelly. Early in the day is usually a good time to catch him because he hasn't started drinking yet. I want him to drive me to town so that I can look for books or magazines written in English, which is the only language I have any ability to read even though I was born in

Greece. Then again, if I spoke Greek, no one in the festival would be able to talk to me at all, a situation that might not always be so bad. At least that way, I'd never understand Rictus and he'd never understand me when I grumble about him like I sometimes can't help.

Leaving the midway, I wander toward the festival's traveling village and Skelly's ugly white trailer. I pass in amongst a few tents and RVs, and I find him tucked on the edge of town, so to speak, in a fetal position on the ground beside his metal doorstep.

"Hey, Skelly," I say, looking down on him.

He opens his eyes and stares at my shoes, which are bare and dirty.

"I know them ain't Maia's feet," he grumbles. "She don't ever wear shoes."

"Wrong," I tell him.

He rubs the wrinkled looking skin on his head. Clearly, he's in the process of fighting off a hangover that, from the way he grimaces, must be sending invisible screws into his temples. "What can I do for ya, me love?"

I squat down and look at him and find myself struggling not to laugh. He looks so bad that no one can look so bad without faking. He's got mud on one cheek, two little yellow worms in his hair, and his clothes are wrinkled.

I ask, "You think we can go to town? I really need a new book because I can't read *The Captain's Soul Mate* anymore. I finally gave up last night after he swung her on a vine over a deep canyon, and she held onto his neck and talked about how he smelled like stone and flint. Can you believe it? Nobody smells the smell of anybody when they're swinging on a vine two hundred feet above the ground. I know that, and I've never even done it."

"Tripe," Skelly mumbles.

"It's definitely cow stomach." I grin at him. "Can we go?"

"Sure… we can, Love. Just got to find the inspiration to rise and shine and get on with me day." He sits up, and I notice that one of his eyes is so bloodshot it looks as if someone sprinkled cayenne pepper into it. "Just you allow me to go tell Rictus so's I don't get accused of trying to fly the coop with ya."

I look at him. "Why would anyone try to fly the coop with me? Can you imagine if Rictus caught someone trying to take me away? He'd probably kill them."

"Sure enough. Ya are his silk purse, ain't ya? Ya are his big money freak." He stands, groaning like he's been stretched on a rack for five or six hours. Patting himself down, he seems surprised that he's all in one piece, like his legs might be one place and his ears another.

When I was young, including the time I ran away, I wondered if Skelly's kindness was real or if he was faking for some reason. Anymore, though, I don't worry about it. First, he's been too nice for too long. Second, I don't believe that a man as outright lazy as he is would do so much if he didn't really care.

"I'm off," he says, and staggers along, his hands dug deep into the pockets of his smelly tweed jacket that is decorated with about a dozen dry leaves and a few small twigs.

I wander over to the trucks and wait. My hair rises toward the sun, as if it's warming itself like a cold blooded animal. Because I'm embarrassed by what it's doing, I command it to lie down, but it refuses to budge. "You're a pain," I tell it, because I often think of myself like a Siamese twin, like my hair is a separate creature from me, and I'm only partially in control.

Weird.

I'm weird.

Skelly returns and tells me that Rictus will allow me to go if I wear a disguise and control my hair.

"Look," I tell Skelly, "I already brought my hat."

"Then let's bust out of here, child," he says, his tender eyeball like a glowing red porch light.

In the truck, Skelly leans over the steering wheel as if he's got a cruel stomach bug. I envision a real insect in his stomach, something like the thumb-sized beetle I found dead in Spain over the winter. I imagine its spinning circles and creating whirlpools of stomach acid. Sometimes, I wonder if Skelly is trying to drink himself to death, which gets me nervous for him and me.

He burps, his whole chest heaving.

"Are… are you going to throw up, you think?"

"Ah… no, dolly. First things first, though. I… I got to find me a spot of beer and a couple espressos to drink, don't ya know?"

In town, we park the truck and wander into a little café, where Skelly gets a large beer and three little coffee drinks that are so thick that grains sit in the bottom of the cup when he's done. Then we go walking, the two of us. We go past an amazing, slightly dark looking church with frightening gargoyles on it. We continue along to a shopping district where I stop in a news shop that sells a couple of English magazines that I don't ever read because I find them boring. On the cover of one is a girl in a bathing suit sticking her behind to one side so that despite her pretty face her spine looks crooked, which is sad if it's true. The other cover has a photo of dozens of Chinese people, including kids, half sinking on a raft in the middle of a blowing ocean. The words above them say, "What to do About the Boatpeople?"

I've never even heard of one boatperson much less a whole group. I look closer and wonder if maybe that type of person lives on overloaded, half-sunk rafts, eating fish and drinking salt water. Because it doesn't seem possible, and they look so desperate, I decide they want to get off the boat, which is really terrible except that the photographer must be on a boat and floating nearby. I kind of figure after he took his picture, he went over and picked them up. At least I hope.

We walk some more and stop in a restaurant. At the bar, Skelly orders a couple more beers. Gulping them back, he says he's beginning to feel better. But I don't know how. I can't imagine needing something as bad as he needs alcohol. His drinking reminds me that dolphins, which can only hold their breath for six or seven minutes, always have to return to the surface to breathe. They can't ever just go roam around exploring the seafloor and come back for air whenever they get bored. They've got no freedom and might as well be chained to a buoy on the surface. Skelly's the same way. He needs liquor like they need air, and he hardly has any freedom from it.

Hours pass, and eventually we return to camp with two books. One is about a gigantic, man-eating shark. It's called *Jaws* and looks exciting. The other is missing its dust jacket, but I like its name, *On the Road*. When I first picked it up, I hoped it was about a girl living in a sideshow like me, but it's not. Instead, it's about a guy named Salvadore Paradise who goes on long trips across America without any money. I'm familiar with not having money, so I got it.

Rictus demands to look at both books. Picking his teeth, he says, "I don't suppose these will give you wild ideas about your place in this sideshow, will they? Keep them. What the hell do I care?"

"You shouldn't care at all," I say softly.

"What?" he asks, rising.

"She didn't say nothing," Skelly tells him, and pulls me away.

I leave the dining tent, say, "Goodbye," to Skelly, and go back to my trailer, excited to read how the shark wants to eat people. I picture it snapping Rictus' big head clear off of his body, and I laugh out loud.

In my trailer, I read for a while before checking the time. I dog-ear my page and meekly do what I hate most in all the world. I make myself look like the freak that lives just beneath my skin. I dress like a monster.

Leaving, I pass slowly through the outskirts of the carnival.

In the distance, as I approach the midway, I feel the way I do whenever we've just relocated, excited. I can see the tents lined up, some of the rides getting tested, and the headless lady with her head solidly attached to her neck. She's leaning against a booth with a banner of Rictus over it.

I see the hoop lady with her rings and top hat. Beyond her is the snake charmer, his bald head shining like cut and polished stone. There's the knife thrower's station and the trapeze artists' tents.

Behind all of that, seated in a chair, is the wolf man already dressed in his matted rabbit-hair suit. He's drinking coffee and smoking a cigarette, and I wonder if a stray ash might set his animal outfit on fire one day. He's kind of a nice guy, so I hope not.

Above the fortune teller's large tent, the empty Ferris wheel is turning and clattering against the beautiful, late afternoon sky. I love moments like this. The midway is empty except for a few of the show's grisly looking carnies rushing about, checking booths, stalls, and tent stakes. I see the fat lady sitting on a bench and eating a knockwurst and roll. Mustard is dripping onto her dress, which Rictus had made to look like the fabric of an old tent because he thinks it makes her appear bigger and fatter and like the only clothes that fit her have to be made from threadbare giant tents.

Shortly, the festival will open and people will funnel down the midway, looking for entertainment.

I veer into my tent, pass by the center pole and arrive at my cage, where I lean against the long wooden planks and stare distractedly into the distance.

I scan the space and my eyes stop on a different Rictus poster. It's plastered about the sides of my tent. On it, it says "Rictus the Amazing," and lists his various accomplishments, or lies, like how he was a crocodile hunter, an Indian fighter, the world's foremost magician, a heavyweight boxing champ, a trained hypnotist, an alpine explorer, a Buddhist monk, a weapons expert, and a classicist (which is someone who studies mythologies, like the myth of Medusa). The thing is, since I've spent my entire life with him, you'd think I might have heard him discussing one of those subjects aside from Medusa. But I haven't, making me think he's actually made it all up. Then again, who's going to question him to his face? He holds everyone's earnings for them, which really means he keeps it. On top of that, there's a slim chance he's a weapons expert and a professionally trained fist fighter, too.

I close my eyes for a few minutes, and when I open them the sweetest yellow bird flies into my tent and circles the high ceiling like a winged dart.

Softly, I say, "Calm down girl. It's okay. It's okay." The bird does a series of strange circles in the air, like the way a child scribbles on paper, and lands on my cage. It chirps at me, its eyes like rivets in its tiny, tiny head. Snapping its beak, it tilts its gaze like it might see me better if I'm at an angle.

"No, you're not trapped in here. You can leave out the same place you came in. See, it's just right over there." I wave some strands of hair in the right direction.

The bird glances back and squeaks at me.

"Oh, these? These come off, sweetie," I tell her and remove my dark glasses. "See that? I'm just a fake monster. I dress this way because I have to."

We stare at each other for a while without making a sound. It's nice to have someone around. I lower a tress of hair and stroke the bird's tiny head. I wonder how it would feel to simply fly away. I wonder how it would be not to have any boundaries at all and soar over Europe like a miniature rocketship. Then I wonder if I might be lonely if I was all by myself that way. Then again, maybe birds don't have any friends. Or maybe all song birds are friends with each other so that they never feel lonesome. Or maybe all birds are friends excluding mockingbirds and crows, who hate each other. I've seen it myself.

I flinch when I hear the sound of people, dozens of them, approaching. Most of them are German. Some are British. Some are American. I have good hearing is why I can tell. Plus, Brits and Americans sound so different. I stare at the bird and hear the rumble and pop of the Ferris wheel gears. I can hear the helium tank expanding balloons like somebody sighing as loud as they can. The popcorn machine is exploding frantically. The smell of knockwurst and bratwurst, bread, and kuchen (the German word for cake), wafts in the air.

I smile.

I hope I haven't given the impression that I hate everything about my life. I don't. In fact, I seldom hate it as much as wish parts of it were different, like Rictus. And on nights like tonight, I can really like it. I like the excitement, the sounds, and the weird mix of smells, and I feel sad for young people who've never been Medusa's Daughter in the Festival de Tordré.

"If you don't like people," I tell the little bird, you better fly away."

It chirps at me.

"I can here them coming."

The bird whistles and chirps and takes flight. It does a ragged, bumpy loop directly over my cage before it veers down and rockets right through the entrance way of my tent.

Beyond my tent, I see the lights of the midway sizzling against the sky, reflecting against tent fabric and signs.

I climb into my cage, which is covered with a banner of me, and pull the back shut so that it appears locked.

Momentarily, Skelly enters. Clearly, he's very drunk. "Maia?" he calls.

"Yeah?"

"Ya ready for a big show?"

"I wish you weren't drunk," I tell him.

"Ya and me both, girl."

Like a dam has burst and water is rushing into a valley, people start to enter.

Skelly climbs atop his little box and holds his hands in the air as if he's presenting something spectacular, like a president or the Queen Mother of England. I can also hear all of the breathing, all of the conversations.

Skelly declares, "Welcome, Ladies and Gentlemen and wee ones of all ages. Welcome to the Festival de Tordré's most amazing attraction!" he yells, striking his cane against the wood and chain link fencing of my cage.

I snarl in the animal sounding way that I can.

Silence spreads through the tent.

Skelly says, "Gather about, mates and lasses, members of America's valiant armed forces. Gather about to see tha dreaded creature that our very own Rictus Fitch, at great risk to his own life and limb, saved from the terrible grip of the fabled Aegean Sea…"

He goes on and on and eventually gets to, "So without further ado, let me present, Medusa's Daughter!" The banner is whipped back and hundreds of eyes focus on me. I glower back and crawl oddly about my cage, my locks lashing about the boards and fencing.

People gasp, which is nice.

Slowly, I stretch my hair through the wooden slats of the cage, then draw it back.

The audience takes a step to the rear.

"Oh, my God!" I hear an older woman with an American accent say as she waddles through the entrance. She waves for someone to hurry. "Come look at this, Diddly, dear. Hurry."

Diddly, if that's his name, pushes his big way forward, and I see he's dressed in an American army officer's uniform. On his left chest, in the area over his heart, is a patch of decorative military badges and pins that look like a bad puzzle.

"Look at her," the lady directs.

Diddly stops and gawks. Then he shakes his block head. "It's done with strings, dear, like the way people manipulate puppets."

"Naw it isn't," she says. "I can tell."

Diddly slips through ragged waves of guests and approaches me, his mouth slightly open so that I can see all of his gold fillings sparkle. He stoops and watches my hair move, his eyes similar to two black jewels below a fantastically unattractive military buzz cut. His skin is rashy and highlighted by pink acne bumps. There are two chunky rings on two chunky fingers, and a teeny zit is growing in the crease beside his face and nostrils. "Well, look at you," he says to me.

Like a dart, I send some locks through the fencing. I want him to think I'm trying to lasso his neck.

He does. He leaps backwards as if I've thrown a pie at him, like in a funny movie. Gulping for air, he backs up all of the way to the lady he's with. "Oh, she's real, all right!" he tells her. "She's real. I'll wager she'd of strangled my neck if I wasn't quick." He rubs the fatness under his chin, the part called a waddle.

Skelly laughs and says, "Step up! Step up! See the beasty. See the myth, but watch yourself. That hair of hers can be a might bit cunning, yes sir. It wants ya. It always wants."

That's how endless days pass into grinding weeks. The cool, late summer air gives way to the nighttime chill of early fall, so that if ever Skelly drinks till he passes out, it's important that he wake up and crawl into his trailer, or he might freeze to death. When I tell him that, though, he says, "I'm fine, Maia, love. I keep a blanket under me trailer, and I already cut back on the drink just to be careful."

I try to remember one single time when he actually drank less, but I can't. "Are you sure you're fine, Skelly?"

He stares at me and smiles. He plucks the side of his head with a finger and plays like it nearly unlatches it from his neck. "I'm okay."

"Are you an alcoholism?"

"Do you mean, do I have alcoholism?"

"Yeah."

"I believe so, yeah." He moves his jaw around like somebody just punched him in it. "But, I got reasons, love, for the things I do. I got my reasons, and they'd drive the president of the United States to the bottle. They'd knock the bloody pope to his knees."

"It doesn't matter," I tell him. "Just be careful you don't freeze to death at night. Okay?"

"I really do keep a blanket underneath me trailer, dear. I'll be fine."

I touch a finger to my lips, wondering how a liquid, like water or Coca-Cola, can cause an adult to become so child-like and babyish that they're unable to save themselves from freezing. It almost seems like black magic, like something from a story with a witch in it.

5
JUST A GIRL IN MAKEUP

It's early morning, and the mayor and an assortment of police officers unexpectedly visit the festival grounds with a list of complaints. Rictus finds this shocking because Rictus believes himself above the law. When he arrives anywhere, he calls himself the Ambassador and carefully goes out to greet local politicians, whom he pays off in advance to ignore the sideshow's unlawful behavior. Also, if he happens to break the law, his payoffs ensure that he won't ever be charged.

Unfortunately, Wadern's town leaders don't see it that way. Maybe they've taken his money and decided to come down on him anyway. Or maybe the Festival de Tordré is far more crooked than they ever imagined. Either way, this morning they declare that the Festival de Tordré is swarming with pickpockets, highwaymen, and illegal poker games, which is all true.

The Ambassador, of course, denies everything. "No," he declares, overacting, "not us."

The police captain explains, "We have conducted an investigation, Herr Fitch. There were undercover officers in your midst for the last few weeks."

Rictus rolls his eyes. "That hurts," he says, even though it sounds as if he's not hurt. "I'm injured by your suggestion. Captain, didn't I personally come to see you so that there wouldn't be any misunderstandings?"

"Ja," he says, which is German for "yes."

Rictus continues. "I told you how I run my show. I told you that I do not allow horribly unlawful behavior in the Festival de Tordré, didn't I?"

The officer says, "No, I don't recollect, dis."

Ambassador Rictus frowns and turns to the bürgermeister, which is the "mayor" in English. Rictus lowers his eyes to give himself the look of a long-haired goblin. Furious, spitting, he says, "Tell me, sir, why do the police officers on your force lie so blatantly?"

Stepping back, the bürgermeister says, "I don't know that they do."

Rictus replies, "You don't, do you? Well you better look into it. Seems to me they are terrible liars. Here your captain has the nerve to take a bribe then come out here and tell me we're breaking the law. And who says that we are? He would pit the sincerity of his undercover officers against my own wonderful reputation as a businessman and entertainer?"

The captain grins. "They took photographs."

"Ah, photographs." Rictus laughs aloud. His greasy, silver hair trembles and bends against his shoulders, while his hard eyes stay fixed on his guests, especially the mayor. "Photographs? Well, they lie, too. Taken at specific angles, any dinner gathering can resemble a casino. Am I correct? Should I, captain, be concerned that you are trying to blackmail me for more money? Is that your game?"

"No," the officer assures him. But the man turns red.

Rictus lowers his blazing gaze on the mayor, who is dressed in old-time German clothing, including a large, heavy sweater and a felt hunting hat. He looks like a bürgermeister.

"Bürgermeister," Rictus says suddenly, "you know as well as I that we would never sully the reputation of our fine family entertainment by gambling or petty thievery. We are not driven by money here, that is why I was so generous when I visited your office quite a few weeks back. Besides, it seems that money is worth nothing these days. You and the good law officer take it and refuse to give fair payment in exchange. In this region of Germany, money has apparently lost its buying power."

"Oh, Herr Fitch, do not be confused, it still has the ability to change minds," the mayor tells him. "But sometimes it requires a series of two equal payments where one was originally believed sufficient."

Rictus looks almost ridiculously scary, like he might lunge at the man and push him to the ground. "Whatever you say, Mr. Mayor... But here's something you should know. I stay out of gambling for very specific reasons."

I almost laugh at his statement. He doesn't stay out of gambling at all.

The bürgermeister says, "And what are they, Herr Fitch?"

"It's a dangerous business."

The bürgermeister nods. "And what's dangerous about it, Herr Fitch?"

"The violence. People always end up dead."

The police captain unbuckles the leather strap on his holster. "Are you making a threat, Herr Fitch?"

Rictus grins. "It wasn't a threat. It was an observation of fact."

"Then go observe your facts away from here," the captain states coldly.

And the confrontation comes to an end. They give the Ambassador, our fair Rictus, three options. He can pack up and leave by nightfall. He can make a second payment to those whom he originally paid off. Or, he can go to jail.

Rictus, who loves money and seems to fear jail at least as much as he fears anything else, decides he'll leave. Within a few hours, the tents are collapsed inwards from their center poles, my cage is folded, and the various stalls are taken apart and placed inside trucks. It's a long process, especially the Ferris wheel, but Rictus pushes the carnies and everyone else. As a result, we finish by late-afternoon and slowly pull out.

I sit locked in my trailer while our caravan snakes up a series of bumpy and very narrow German roadways that our American trucks and automobiles overwhelm like whales in a swimming pool. Rictus likes that. He enjoys forcing people to the curb so that they can see the big American sideshow pass by.

We travel slowly, our progress hindered by wrinkly farmers atop horse-drawn wagons and herds of black and white goats that look like dogs with curled horns. None of them seem in a hurry. I sit on my seat cushions and watch my hair play games with two flies. Once, a strand mimics a lasso, twirls in a circle, then rushes out and snags a fly like it's a big steer in an American Western movie. Another time it simply snatches them both out of the sky without any effort. A third time, it shoots across the room and grabs one by its two clear wingtips. It goes on that way, and I eventually look back out and daydream.

An hour or two later, we are snaking down a high ridge that is cluttered with fallen rocks and tall trees in a forest with little underbrush. The trees around us slowly give way to a cliff then the most beautiful bronze wheat fields that dart out in rows that look like hundreds of narrow "welcoming" carpets disappearing into the distant Rhineland.

The caravan wobbles along the edge of a cliff, where, at the bottom sits a tremendous, rocky outcrop encircled by a dark green field that is the tint of the English Channel during a storm. The rock, which is like an island or volcano, has deep overhangs and cracked gray walls, reminding me of a fantastic castle from the book *The Lion the Witch and the Wardrobe*, where the evil White Witch lives and keeps all of her victims frozen. It's been a long time since I read the story. But I imagine myself on top of the high tower of stone, leading an army in a long, flowing dress that has a nice bright pattern. I also have a sword at my side and my hair is waving like that Hindu god Shiva with all the arms.

In the valley, we cruise alongside a train track. I look above it and enjoy the tall, chimney-like white clouds that are glowing yellow in the horizontal sun. I think of a painting where God comes down to earth in a cloud to make Adam or Moses or somebody else.

Then a train roars by as if it has a rocket buckled to it. It seems like it's barely staying on the tracks. I watch it pass and feel the urge to ride. We slow, take some turns that are difficult for the big trucks in our caravan, and come to a stop outside of a town named Göllheim. I swing my feet around to stand, and as my eyes pass across the carpeting, I see the two flies from the start of my trip. They are settled on the floor an inch or so apart. They're dead. It's crazy, but I feel terrible about it. I feel as if my evil hair has tortured two noble creatures to death.

I put the flies in my hand and wait for someone to unlock my trailer's door. Out my windows, I can see people unloading trucks and the distant figure of Rictus pointing out where to place certain tents. Eventually, Horst arrives.

"Demon!" he yells at me. But it's always funny hearing that from him. He was the Nazi youth, a boy who marched through

Berlin holding a burning torch and hating Jews and everyone who didn't see the same way he did. He was the kid who carried the Nazi flag at the front of the parade and probably thought that one day doing so would make him an important and powerful leader instead of a sad, overweight strongman in a sideshow. He got what he deserved.

"Evil thing," he tells me, removing the padlock and walking away.

I breathe deep and go out to bury the insects. On my knees, I am about to drop them into a shallow grave beside my trailer's steps, when the two bugs suddenly buzz against my hand and fly away. It's the strangest thing. I can't even begin to figure it out and wonder if my hair might have hypnotized them.

"Wow," I say, like a proud parent. I'm just so glad that my hair was kinder than I thought it might be. I reach up and touch moving locks, and they wrap around my hand like a caring snake.

Weeks drift by. Or maybe it is only two weeks. Or maybe only a few days. I've started losing track of time. Sometimes I leave the show thinking it's light out and it's dark. Sometimes it's the other way around. Outside of Göllheim, where we're located, the weather turns chillier. Except for the growing cold, it's hard to remember where we are on the calendar.

Göllheim is small, but the residents overwhelm us, as if they've been choking of thirst and we're water. It's the most amazing time I've ever experienced in the Festival de Tordré.

As always, visitors respond to me in different ways. Certain folks want a quick glimpse. Others want to stand and stare all night. Some don't ever leave my tent. A few folks want to set me free, others want to hurt me because I'm so unnatural. It's been the same way for years. And I'm still terrible at judging who's thinking what.

A thousand faces huddle and pass. Shows come and go in a blur. Images of various visitors linger while others disappear in an instant. Three nights in a row I get back to my trailer worried I'm freezing to death. I begin to feel the urge to head south for the Mediterranean, where it's still warm. I miss the southern coast of Europe, which is understandable, I guess, since I was born on a warm weather island.

It's late. Tonight a beautiful young girl stands in front of my cage, while others glare at me from a distance. The girl's about my age. Her smile is full but slightly crooked. She has the tiniest, most heartbreaking scar on her bottom lip and is wearing a beautiful, warm dress while my nearly bare skin is covered in goose bumps so big she must think I have a skin disease. I shake my head gently. I love how the girl's thin eyebrows are cocked like identical pen marks on paper.

I find myself wishing I looked like her. I wonder what her life is like, if she has a nice home and parents, soft bed covers, drawers of clothes, a bicycle. I've always wanted a bicycle. Better yet, does she have girl friends? Is she dating a handsome boy? I wish I could ask, but I'd never dare say a word. I'm far too scared of Rictus.

What I know is that the girl must be happy.

She slides around to the side of my cage, where it's nothing but splintery boards. She's holding a pencil, and I wonder if she wants to give it to me. If she does, I'd like to have it. I'd like anything of hers, hoping she might rub off on me, that I might wake up and find myself gentle, well-dressed, a young woman. Besides, she can afford to be generous since she probably has everything she's ever wanted.

She says, "Hergekommen, Medusa. Hergekommen. Nicht nicht gerade dein haar. Du."

I think she wants me to come closer to her, so I slither forward and lean against the boards of my cage.

The girls creaseless brow knits. Her lovely teeth show because she's snarling. She pivots and stabs at me with the pencil, driving it into my shoulder.

I fall backwards, my entire arm on fire. I roll in the hay and hiss at the girl.

She smiles.

She has everything, and she feels the need to hurt me. Why?

A blindness overtakes me. I see but don't see. It's as if my brain is wired incorrectly.

I roll over and scamper to my feet. Then I leap at her, my hair lashing out and catching the lovely cuff of her dress sleeve, which it pulls and tears. Another thick strand takes the pencil from her in an instant, latching tightly to her forearm. A third searches for her neck. I want her neck. I want to do something terrible.

I screech so loudly that the girl bursts into tears. I send another cable of black hair lunging for her, and it pulls off a locket that dangles delicately around her throat. Someone strikes at my cage with a chair, as if I'm a lion. But I'm not a lion. I could crush a lion.

Outside, somebody struggles to free the girl, whose wrist I have tightly bound. A man sticks a broom handle in a slat and pushes at me. I break it.

Then I hear someone named Skelly. "Maia. Maia. Back away. Let her go, love."

I'm so furious that I've lost the ability to speak. I'm an animal with an animal's confused brain.

"Maia, deary, let her go! Let go!" the person named Skelly pleads.

The beautiful girl has fainted. People, grown men, are trying to pull her free.

In a blink, and, like a lightning strike, I am me and realize what's going on, that I'm wrestling with four grown men over the unconscious form of the girl who stabbed me in the shoulder.

I release her and fall back into the hay. I can't stand myself, who I am, what I am becoming. My shoulder throbs where the pencil went in, and I stare at the top of my cage and wish that I was a bird who could fly away to a distant island.

Skelly rushes around, squats and whispers, "Jesus, child, what happened to ya?"

I turn away from the crowd. Distantly, I rasp, "I became the evil me."

"But what happened?" he says again.

I show him my shoulder and the bloody burlap fabric of my Medusa clothes. "She stabbed me in the arm for no reason. She told me to come close, and she stabbed me with a pencil."

"That little weasel."

I shake my head. "Still… I shouldn't have gone after her."

Skelly gets closer. His dragon breath punishes my sense of smell. "That's your opinion, love, not mine."

I can't imagine what will happen to me.

I can't imagine what Rictus will do.

I don't sleep at all. Instead, I reread *Jaws*. That's a monster who deserved what he got. My situation isn't very similar. I was stabbed in my shoulder.

It's midday now, and Rictus informs me that no one is filing charges. I won't get into trouble. There were three dozen witnesses who saw her stab me. Skelly says the girl also has a history. She's not nice. Recently, she did something to a neighbor's cat. A year ago someone accused her of killing a cow in a field with a pitch fork. People say that her conscience is missing, that she's sick. Aren't I the same way, though?

Rictus warns me, though. "You will never, ever, do that again."

I nod.

So I'm back on display, snarling at visitors, doing tricks with my hair. Days slip past. Again, I don't know how many. The injured part of my shoulder doesn't heal quickly. It aches in the cold air. The crowds, though, they grow even larger. After what

I've done to the girl, after holding back four adult men, nobody in the area will ever doubt that I'm their worst nightmare, Medusa's Daughter, the heir to the throne, a killer.

Another few weeks, and I wake up to frost on the ground. I go out to look at it, and a raccoon is standing by the door to my trailer, balanced on its hind legs.

"Yes, sir?" I ask, like it can understand me.

It lowers back to its forelegs.

I tell it, "I don't have any fish."

It doesn't budge.

I go back inside, get a sweater for myself and a piece of cheese, which I carry out and hand over to the raccoon.

It takes it from me and gnaws away with its needle shaped teeth. When it's finished, it chirps at me and ambles off towards the woods.

I watch till it's gone, then I sit on my trailer step and hold my knees together like most of the smart looking German girls I see visiting the sideshow. It's a beautiful day. Shafts of early fall light streak the dark ringlets of my hair, and the irregular shadows of leaves tremble on the surface of my pants' legs and bare feet. I smile to myself, comfortable, for the moment, with who I could be if I ever left the Festival de Tordré.

I sit there for a while before the romantic, soothing feel of the morning slips away. When it's time to let it go, I step back into my trailer to read before I wash my sack cloth dress for the afternoon and evening shows.

Hours slip away. I go for a walk. I play volley ball against my trailer. Late afternoon comes and the first show begins.

Now it's night. Skelly, feeling like a showman, jumps on his box and hollers about how awful I am. It's his typical prepared speech, but he's delivering it with more spark. Still, I've heard it all before, thousands of times. He says, "Truth be told, we don't know much about this beast, but we all heard the rumors!

Odysseus stumbled upon her during his journey back from the Trojan War! Perseus cut off her head. She was a disgusting sight back then! A tragic beast! A horrible, soulless monster! Now behold, blokes," he whips off the covering that hides me, "see MEDUSA'S DAUGHTER!"

I rush the fencing. My writhing bands of hair shake it. My dirty hands take hold of the mesh, and I play like I'm trying to tear it free of its anchors.

The audience, with all of its pale faces, jumps back.

Skelly shouts, "Note tha monster's glasses, ladies and gentlemen—fraus and herrs. If ever she gets a good look at ya, ya'll turn to stone. I seen it happen to a lad of six or seven only last year!"

I almost laugh.

Skelly bellows, "She's a terrible, awful sight! A cruel hard predator with a taste for blood and a love of the chase!"

An elderly lady wearing a cross around her neck approaches the front of my cage, stops and looks very closely at me. She speaks in German to the miserable looking people behind her. All I understand is the word "gemein," which means filthy. I send a lock of hair out between the fencing to scare her, and she screams joyfully and rushes away laughing.

People are weird.

Others gather around, including a large American man who tells Skelly, "She don't look so tough."

Skelly gets down from his platform and places a hand atop my cage. "Captain, she broke our strongman's hand when she was nary nine. Wasn't no effort at all. I'd wager she'd snap that pencil arm of yours in about two seconds flat... or less."

I fire out a bolt of hair and thump the American hard in his hip.

Caught by surprise, he stumbles sideways, whips about, and studies me.

"I'm warning ya, she's a wee bit sinister," Skelly tells him as the crowd cracks up.

My hair rises and hisses at him, and, in response, he takes about three big steps back. "She bothers me," he says.

"Imagine if she took off them glasses. That stone business is an ugly thing ta experience."

Skelly waits a minute, then he jumps back on his box and theatrically throws his arms wide. "Come one, come all, come see Medusa's Daughter! View the creature from the myth, the child of the monster whose eyes created the Atlas Mountains, whose blood solidified the coral reefs of the Red Sea! Come and know the menace of a gorgon!"

The crowd is silent.

Then someone slips to the front. She's wearing a scarf around her head and holds a little purse. On her ears are tiny pearl earrings that I don't like the style of. Her hair is pulled back tightly. Obviously, she's German, and I wonder what she could possibly be doing at the Festival de Tordré. She doesn't look like the type who would enjoy a crummy American sideshow or some secretive gambling.

"Bitte," she says to me, which is how German's say "please." The woman stumbles toward me on legs that appear tired from work, weather, time and not the greatest stockings.

Skelly continues to announce me.

The lady calls softly, "Child? Little One!" and kneels in front of my cage.

The crowd starts to hum with activity.

Her mouth is open, as if she's in a low state of shock. "Mein got!" she says. "Maia? Is that you?"

I'm shocked to hear my name come from the woman's mouth.

Beside me, Skelly stops shouting. "Oh, Jesus, Joseph, and Mary, it's a blasted ghost!" he hisses. His face appears drained of blood.

Trembling, the woman asks me, "Maia? Maia? Is that you?"

I wonder again how she knows me.

"Maia, child, you are no monster! You are just a girl in makeup."

Above, Skelly, who looks as if he's just seen a vision of his own tombstone, lurches forward, leans and shouts at the woman, "Stop! Don't get near the beast, lady! Sie ist das biest!" he repeats in German. "She's not tame!"

Time seems to slow.

My arms lower. There's a quality to the aging lady. My gaze is drawn to hers, where it stays and doesn't waver. Her old eyes grow wide and full of sadness and sympathy. I can't tell if she's horrified or hopeful. Either way, she's crying. Looking at me has caused her to cry.

Overhead, Skelly continues to yell. "Get away from her, hag!" he demands. "For your own good, back away, or I'll call security!"

I want to talk to the lady, but Rictus' rules are in the way. I have a sense for how dangerous it would be to disobey him. Too dangerous, I suppose.

My heart is working so hard it's shaking the fangs loose in my mouth. The woman touches old fingers to the chain link separating us. "Oh, my child, I… I knew a girl… I knew a Fräulein like you. I knew her eleven years ago. Her name vas Maia? Maia Gasol? Is… that you, Maia Gasol, dear? Is dis you?"

Skelly starts pounding his cane atop my cage. Do not speak to the monster," "Security! Somebody get security!"

Even if I was allowed to speak, I wouldn't know what to say. It's as if we're moving slowly in water, so that every flinch of our hands and movement on our faces appears to stretched out for a long time.

"Maia Gasol had hair like yours," the lady says.

I reach for her hand. It's got big veins and some reddish spots on it. Still, I want to put my fingers in hers, to feel her warmth or coldness.

Then the crowd separates. Horst and Willem have arrived and are acting as if they are saving me from the woman. Horst, wearing his big leather bracers, looks arrogant, serious, and intimidating. Willem just appears big and puppet-like, as if he's not exactly sure what he's doing.

The two come forward, and the lady pivots about and yells, "Nein! Nein!" meaning "no" in German. When they grab her under the arms, they yank her back and away roughly. She shouts and extends a hand toward me, but Horst and Willem are strong and used to bullying people twice her size.

When she disappears out of the tent, I jump up and down similar to monkeys I've seen in zoos. I slam a fist against the ceiling and screech in anger.

The crowd thinks it's all an act. A few people even start to clap.

My hair and hands latch against the fencing. I want Horst and Willem to bring her back, but I can't talk, not a word.

In frustration, my hair writhes about looking for an object to bend and break. I hear something crunch like a car against a tree, and, turning, I realize that a coil has hurled my metal water dish against the back wall of my cage.

I want to know who Maia Gasol is. I want to know if we're cousins or sisters. I want to know if she really has hair like mine.

From the hands of an American serviceman, a soda bottle somersaults toward me, crashing against my cage. He either hates me or thinks I'm a mindless animal suffering rabies like the dog in *Old Yeller*, which is a good American story about a nice dog that has to be killed due to his bad luck of catching rabies.

I shake my head, furious at the people around me. Steadily, my personality slides away, and once more I am somebody or something else. I screech harshly and slam against the chain link door, trying to tear it free, trying to seize the callous GI who threw the bottle at me.

Skelly tells me to stop, but I extend a hair and shove him aside. He turns, leans, and drops the banner advertising my act over my cage. "Folks," he declares, breathing heavily, "we gotta be civilized here, huh! We gotta be friendly to the abomination. The old lady stirred her up."

In the shadows, I slump forward, my hair continuing to bang away at the cage like I've got access to a sledge hammer. Wham! Wham! I start to cry. I can't help it. I want to shake Skelly for calling Horst and Willem over. Wham! Wham! I want to scream in his face for having the old woman dragged away from my tent.

I bury my head in an arm. Time passes. Wham! Wham! I can feel the tips of my hair, and they hurt. But the pain helps me concentrate. I hate this place. I hate it. And, it seems, the serpents that possess my hair do, too.

It's late. Skelly has finished our third show. Atel stands nearby, his unkind face dour like he's broken a tooth on a ham bone, and I hope he has. The mural in front of my cage is pulled back so that those remaining at the carnival can stare at me as they pass. I don't care. My mind feels clouded by images of the old woman who spoke the name Maia Gasol.

After all of our visitors are gone, I exit through the back of my cage, my knees and elbows sore from the way I slammed against the wooden slats. My palm is cut by a sharp edge from the water-bowl. No one is around, which is good because I don't want to see anyone.

Walking, I think of the elderly woman, her veiny hands, the scarf. There was something so unique about her.

The moon is glowing like a frozen steel ball over the cold, distant hills. The Festival de Tordré's lights are dim, the Ferris wheel seems like a delicate etching on the trees and purple atmosphere. It's cold, and steam rises up from my mouth as I walk and shiver, my bare feet crunching across the rocky ground.

At my trailer, I pause and click my throat in a way that is always followed by tears. I wonder if Maia Gasol's parents attempted to drown her, too. Or was that only me?

"Lassy," Skelly is standing in the darkness, his arms at his side, hands in his pockets. He appears to have been frozen in a casket.

"I don't want to talk," I tell him. "Please."

He nods. "Sure. I understand. Ya're mad. But ya gotta know I called for Atel and Horst cause I was worried for ya. Ya know what happened a few weeks back, the girl with the pencil. I had no idea what the old lady wanted. I had no idea, so I had to be cautious."

"I'm freezing," I tell him, opening the door to my trailer and going inside.

"Night, dear," he calls.

Inside, I toss my sack cloth to the floor and change into softer clothes. I turn in a circle. I don't want to sleep. I pick up *Jaws* the book and look into the mirror, which I do more and more. Usually, I wonder if I could be pretty. I don't know. After that, I wonder who I am. But now I wonder who I am first. Growing up in the Festival de Tordré, I've always attempted to rise above my circumstance and be a better person than those who work with me, which isn't hard. Most everyone in the sideshow hates doing what they do and living how they live. They're angry or unhappy, and almost all of them are unfriendly.

Now I'm the angry one. Now I'm the one who hates every aspect of this place.

6

THE PADDY

It's finally morning. I slept poorly.

My hair pushes me to a sitting position. In time, I get out of bed and go to the mirror like I'm obsessed with my looks. But I'm not. I'm still wearing makeup from the night before and it's smeared and hardened.

I wipe my face clean, drape a blanket over my shoulders, and go outside, where I see something strange even for a freak show. Beyond the line of trees, amongst the tents and trailers, are a series of police cars with their lights flashing on and off in the morning sun. Standing beside them are police officers, dressed in impressive uniforms that are so dark and blue they look like holes cut out of the air. They are surrounded by a ragged jumble of folks from the carnival.

I watch for a few minutes, but I can't tell what's going on. Sort of hoping that Rictus is in trouble again, I toss the blanket back into my trailer and walk over to listen. On the way, I force my hair down over my shoulders, where it rests awkwardly, like the hair of a dried paintbrush. When I get to the first line of tents, I'm greeted by the fortune teller, Thespula Dalton, who's never forgiven me for hurting her son, Willem.

Thespula blocks my way, her eyes furious, her curly hair limp against her long face. She sticks a thumb out and indicates the shifting crowds behind her. "Look at the mess you caused."

Confused, I say, "What mess is that?"

Then Rictus brushes through the flaps of his tent followed by a police officer who looks as if he was kissed by a princess and turned into a man who's still partially a frog. His knees seem bent oddly, like he's always about to leap.

Smiling falsely, Rictus says to him, "So we understand ourselves, do we not?" Rictus has a cheerful tone. It's the one he uses when talking to officials he has just paid off.

The officer, who has a pasty, long face, bows his head elegantly. "Yes, we do, Mr. Fitch."

"Wonderful. Then I won't give this business a second thought. Not one." He looks up at the sky that appears clear and blue and so seamless it must be a perfectly woven sheet of silk pulled over a glass dome. Picking a tooth, he says, "It's a lovely day in Göllheim."

"Why, yes, Mr. Fitch, I think you're right," the officer says.

Rictus says, "Sir, I won't give this business any more thought. Not a thought, then."

"To do so would be a waste of time," the officer replies as he gets into his automobile, a Volkswagon Bug with a police light on top. "I'll have to come see the thing in question before too long."

Rictus chuckles. "And you'll come as my guest."

"Why, thank you, Herr Fitch."

The other officers tip their hats before getting into their vehicles and leaving slowly across the field and up a winding road toward town.

Rictus smiles and waves. When they're out of sight, Rictus, whose face heats to a pinky red glow, signals for me to come over. I do, and he keeps smiling like he wants to tell me something funny, except it's not funny at all. Instantly, he clamps a hand around my throat. He stares at me without saying a word, then he touches his nose to mine. "Little Maia, have you not learned! Have I not said it a thousand times?"

"Said what?" Fearing for my life, my hair wraps gently about his wrist but doesn't exert pressure. Looking at his furious face, I'm terror stricken, causing my legs to lose all strength like I can't walk.

"Have you not learned to maintain character while you are playing Medusa!"

I want to say I never broke character.

"Seems, little Maia, you had a long conversation with some senile old lady from town last night. People say that she filled your trembling mind with all sorts of preposterous ideas and that you lapped it up. Well guess what, she called the police on our fine establishment! She called the police because she thinks you were…" He stops short, as if his words have tripped him up. Then, applying pressure to my neck, he says, "She thinks you're some kind of neglected gypsy vagabond. She thinks you need to be saved from us, your keepers. So tell me, WHAT DID YOU TELL HER!"

Voice wavering, I say, "I… I didn't talk. I really didn't say…"

"SHUT UP!" he shouts, suddenly letting me go like he's doing me a great favor, like he's in total control and showing me mercy. He holds his hands out. "We've got witnesses! There were witnesses! Horst and Willem saw you bending the old hag's ear."

Backing into his tent, I shake my head, "I…"

He follows after me and shoves me so that I stumble backwards and fall down.

"I should drag you out of here and leave you on the side of the road, Maia. I should let the other members of this festival poke you with sticks. Do you see what you've done! Do you understand! I'M NOT HAPPY!"

I cover my face and beg to escape from that place, where everyone gets to see him treat me like a family dog that's peed in the house.

"People don't get but one warning when they work for me," he continues, "and I've given you half a dozen over the years. Consider it paternal affection. Consider it love of some sort or another. No matter, dear, there is a breaking point. I have a breaking point! And you have nearly reached it!"

"Sorry," I push along the ground with my feet, trying to create a little distance between me and him. "I am so sorry, Rictus."

Rictus stops. He glowers at me. Then he smiles. When he speaks, he's changed the pitch and edge in his normally icy and mocking voice. He tries to sound like he cares, which he doesn't, making me hate him all the more. He grins the most forced, stupid grin I've ever seen and says, "Oh, Maia, I tell you this for your own good. I do, my love. You are risking your future for no reason." He squats down and brushes my shoulder, which nearly causes me to vomit. I don't want him touching me at all.

Sitting on his heels, he says, "Maia, you have grown so much in the last ten years. You've become a lovely person despite who you really are. But it's my job to keep you working as an employee of the Festival de Tordré. We can't have you looking out for yourself. You can't go asking others for jobs or kindness or anything. We are your family, and you can't go off seeking fame and fortune on your own. Do you understand?"

He's acting ridiculous. For as long as I can recall, he's drilled into my head that everywhere I might go I'd be hated and despised the way I was at birth, when my parents left me on the rock shaped like a winged foot. I nod, though, and realize that my neck is stiff and feels swollen.

Rictus rubs my cheek, stands, and sweeps away like he's handled a serious problem.

Everyone is watching me. I don't want them to.

I rise in front of them. I don't back down, either, like I have before. I can't explain why, but I'm not crying. I'm emotionless, as if his anger has crushed the details of who I am.

Thespula the fortune teller, who's wearing a dark robe embroidered in gold, calls to me, "You're running out of time, Medusa's Daughter. There is a point in the near future where you will no longer have the crutch of the sideshow."

I stop and give her the evil eye, which is a bit like giving the evil eye to a snake. Her lips are thick with nearly black lipstick. They angle down in permanent scorn, while her brows rise up like she's a woodland creature. I'm not afraid of her, though.

I start back to my trailer, through the tents and onto the midway. Swallowing hurts, but I try to ignore it and block the incident from my mind. I don't want to remember Rictus hurting me that way.

I angle for my trailer, tucked into a clearing in the distance, and nearly smack headlong into Skelly, who's running with the floppy, out of control gate of a sock doll or a man whose never run before in his life.

Gasping for air, he stops hard and puts his hands on his knees, then he rises and places a hand on my still trembling shoulders to get a look at my face. "He didn't touch ya, Darling, did he?"

I hesitate. "Some. Just here." I show him my neck.

Eyes wide and injured, he studies the area. "Jesus, Joseph, and Mary. I… I done a sorry job'a watching your back today, Maia. When I heard the shouting, I came fast as me legs would work."

"I can watch out for myself."

"I know. Yeah, I know, girly. But it don't ever hurt to have someone else searching for things ya don't see."

"Sadly, I see it all. I can't help but see it all. It's rubbed in my face is why." I start walking. For some reason, I'm still annoyed with Skelly for calling Horst and Willem over. "Guess what?"

"What?" he asks.

"The lady last night, she called the police on us thanks to Willem and Horst. Plus, Willem and Horst told Rictus I spoke to her, when I didn't. I wish I had now. I got beaten up for not doing anything wrong. Nothing."

Skelly shakes that wrinkled and booze-soaked head of his.

"I didn't say a word to her. And I wanted to. I wanted to ask her a few things and you wouldn't allow it."

He seems to shrink in the morning light, his bleary eyes like two grimy ping pong balls. He throws his hands into the air. "I'm an ass… Okay? I'm an ass, Maia. I shouldn't have done it."

At my trailer, I stop and tell him, "She knew another girl like me? She said her name."

"And what was it?"

"Maia… Maia Gasol."

He looks upward like somebody has just pulled the hair on his neck. Eyes on the sky, he tells me, "Maia Gasol. Never heard that till this minute. Not once till this sorry minute, sweetie."

Exasperated, I say "I didn't expect that you would have heard of her, because if you had, you'd have told me. That's why I wanted to talk to her. That's why it was important. But that's exactly what I didn't do, and I get in trouble anyway." My hair is writhing with energy, and I don't even attempt to control it.

"Would I have told you if I knew her?" he asks.

I tell him, "Yes."

He just looks at me.

"We need to go to town," I announce, "so I can find the woman?"

"Oh, Maia, Rictus ain't gonna let ya leave here, not today, not after last night."

"Tell him I need some books."

"He ain't gonna let ya."

"I do need books. I read the other two."

"It ain't gonna happen, deary."

"Ask. That's all."

"But…"

"Just ask. Just this once."

He digs his hands into his pockets. He looks totally stressed by his circumstance. "Let me go try, lassy, how 'bout?"

"That's all I want."

"Lemme go try," he repeats, pivoting awkwardly and walking off toward Rictus' tent.

7

BRIBED

I sit down and wait for Skelly to return, the sun on my back, the cool German air feeling nice on my exposed arms.

I think about Skelly talking to Rictus, which starts me thinking about Rictus, which is always a bad subject. When I was a child, I was terrified of him and still am. At first, he called himself my father, but I refused to play along, so he made me call him Mr. Fitch. I'd have to say, "Mr. Fitch, this" or "Mr. Fitch that." What I wanted to say was, "Goodbye, Mr. Fitch," and go off somewhere better.

I've witnessed him do awful things to people. Remember Lulu, the World's Smallest Woman? It was humiliating to remake her into the Human Monkey when she already had to deal with being a midget. Even worse than that, though, was the situation I witnessed with a man called Zorba the Human Knob. Zorba had lost half his head during an Allied bombing raid of

Pottsdam, Germany during World War II, which was the reason he was called the Human Knob, because he looked like one. It seemed more than amazing that he was still alive and able to function at all. That's also why Zorba was easily confused. He could lose his way in the tiny trailer he shared with about ten other men, all whom thought he was irritating. Worse, Rictus felt the same way.

Then came the day Zorba attempted to milk all of us like cows. It was the strangest thing, especially when he walked up to Rictus, took a bucket and yelled, "Fill dis bucket, stinky! Fill it now, mädchen!"

"Mädchen," by the way, means girl.

That was the end of the line for Zorba. Over the years, he had misplaced tools, objects, and other items. He constantly mistook carnies for chairs and the fat lady for a severed rhino head. He'd thought the bearded lady was St. Nicholas and Atel was a small rodent. He'd told Horst that he was a dung beetle, and others that they were other things, and once he'd been arrested for going to the bathroom in a phone booth. But he shouldn't have tried to milk Rictus. And he shouldn't have called him a girl.

Rictus had Horst strip Zorba of all his clothes and drive him out into the countryside, where the poor man was left on a snowy back road at the foot of the Alps, which was a death sentence for someone who thought coats were giant leeches. To this day, I wonder whatever happened to the Human Knob?

I've also wondered, what turns a boy into a furious man like Rictus.

What I know about Rictus I've overheard. He grew up in Detroit, Michigan, where he stole lunch money and battered smaller boys for fun. His father, Keeny, supposedly, was worthless, a drunk. Apparently, one day Rictus and Keeny Fitch got in a fight, and Rictus taught his father a lesson by hitting him in the head with a shovel.

After that, he headed out of town, where he was arrested for stealing, trespassing, fraud, assault and battery, assault with a deadly weapon, and attempted murder, as well as other things I can't remember. It was during the trial for the last crime that he escaped police custody and headed down south where he traveled for five years, doing all of the fake and spectacular things he says he did on his posters. Eventually, though, he met the owner of the Festival de Tordré at a cocktail party in Savannah, Georgia. I heard him tell someone, "That man was a card player. He bet it all, everything we owned, and I won the hand and won this sideshow right out from under him. And, ever since, I've made strides to improve it yearly."

However, late one morning, while I was walked back to my trailer, I heard him discussing the matter with Ersatz Irrata, the bearded lady, in the dining tent.

Rictus was laughing softly, before he said, "Ersatz, dear, I came to own this place because I simply didn't give the previous owner, Mr. Farcy, a choice. It was that simple. A person who has taken a violent blow to the head with a shovel blade doesn't usually stay in an argument for long. So, seeing as he appeared quite permanently impaired, I decided it was best for me to take ownership of this sorry carnival and try to save it."

Ersatz told him, "It was doing quite well, Rictus."

"Yes, it was doing well in this country, but we hadn't yet explored the limitless boundaries of Europe. That's why I borrowed all of Mr. Farcy's money, too. Because I knew it was what he would have wanted. Two days later, we boarded that Greek freighter you found so disgusting, and we shipped over here, far, far away from inquiring eyes. And I became the upstanding owner of the Festival de Tordré."

"You were running from the law."

He said, "Yes, I guess one could say that."

"And you've never been upstanding."

"Correct," he snickered.

"And, Rictus, moving us overseas nearly bankrupt us. For nearly a year, we lived like dogs."

"Ah, but Ersatz, we survived." A chair scooted out, and, frightened they might find me, I hurried on my way.

I have never forgotten that conversation. Still, I take it all with a grain of salt. Rictus is such a liar, I'm not sure either story is completely true or if he even knows the truth anymore.

What I know is how much I disdain Rictus.

There was a time, when I was younger, when just seeing him caused me to panic or feel sick. In fact, I got so disgusted with him that one day, I swept a knife off of one of the dining tables and pointed it at him.

Holding it in front of me, I said, "I don't want to stab you. I only want to leave here forever so I can be… happy. I wanna be happy and do happy things."

Rictus stared at me. "If… if that touches me, touches a hair, I will make you wish you were no longer here, girl. I'll make you wish I'd left you to drown."

Thespula Dalton, the fortune teller, put a hand to her head and acted as if she was reading my mind. "She's got no backbone, Rictus. She won't fight back. She's terrified of violence."

"Really?" he asked her.

She said, "Am I not the fortune teller?"

Snickering, Rictus held up his arms to give me a free stab. I remember thinking that he must really think that Thespula could see into my head, because he wasn't one to risk his life for anything. In fact, there are times when he's very much a coward.

For instance, once when we were in Spain, he woke up to find a large spider on his bed sheets, causing him to scream like a truck with bad brakes till the sword swallower came in and killed the thing with a wad of newspaper. Another time, when an armed American soldier came after Rictus for payment on his gambling earnings, Rictus developed a stutter and a lisp that lasted for two months.

So I know he wouldn't have been so brave with a knife in his face under most conditions.

Rictus said, "Take a stab, Maia, but you better do the job in one motion or I will punish you appropriately. Try. Go ahead, waif."

But I didn't want to stab him. I just wanted him to let me leave.

"Brat, let me inform you of something. I control you. I own you. You are nothing without someone leading you by your nose."

I stayed silent while my courage shrunk to the size of a pin tip. Shivering, I continued to hold the point in his direction.

He put out a hand, palm up. "You're a flea," he said softly.

I refused to speak.

"A fly."

I lowered the knife.

"I control you, Maia."

Fear overwhelmed my determination, and I surrendered the knife and my resolve to him.

"Maia," he said, "you're a cat without claws. You're a fool."

Holding one of my elbows, Rictus led me to my trailer. "I'm let down with you," he told me.

I stayed silent.

"I thought I had house trained you a bit better. But now I understand that brutality and animalism permeate your blood, so you should, by all means, live like the creature you are. And I'm willing to give you that."

And he did.

For two straight weeks, I was chained to the front of my trailer. During performances, Horst escorted me from my trailer to my cage. When I was done, it was back to the chain. Rictus made me drink from puddles and sleep on wet hay in front of all of the other carnival workers. By the time I was done, I felt more like an animal. It was disgusting, awful thing to do to an eight-year-old child. I won't forgive it, either. There are certain insults that live between your muscles and your skin, that inhabit you, and that inhabits me.

I walk in a circle. Thirty minutes to an hour passes, but Skelly doesn't return, which scares me. I wonder if Rictus has done something awful to him. I begin to wish I hadn't sent him to beg for me.

I walk in fifty more circles and decide I should go check on him.

Walking slowly, nervously through the midway, I listen for Rictus' voice. When I reach the other side, I stand amidst the performer's tents, where I'm surprised to hear Skelly's instead. He stops and laughs. I slip inside the bearded lady's tent and find him sitting with Ersatz, sharing a bottle of wine.

I stare, feeling sick, as if he has betrayed me. "Skelly… ah… did you go ask Rictus?"

He gapes up at me, embarrassed. "Oh, Maia, dear. Ah, yeah, I was about to and…" He points at me with a wine glass in his hand, but I…" He stops and just stares at me like I'm shining a spotlight in his eyes.

Ersatz, though, has no problem speaking up. She says, "Well, hello, little one, you've had a very rough day, haven't you?"

I don't talk to her.

"Skelly here has been telling me about what happened last night."

I ask, "You mean, about the lady?"

"Oh, but of course. And I'm sure it was very traumatic. But then again, let me enlighten you. I knew a Maia Gasol character, and it's true that she could wiggle a few tiny pieces of hair, but she didn't have coils, girl. She wasn't a killer. She couldn't have shaken a big boy like my Willem nearly to death."

"I didn't mean to hurt him."

She smiles at me. "Whatever, you say. Maia Gasol, dear, was a spoiled child from London who couldn't go to bed at night if she wasn't given her cup of chamomile tea and a crumpet, which makes it all the more funny that bad fortune has seen her become the frumpy, acrid smelling mother of a half-dozen runny-nosed kids. Worse, she's living off the welfare system in Brighton, England. She's a tramp."

"Brighton?" I say.

"It's a beach town."

"She's got kids?"

"Half a dozen."

"Is… Maia old? It didn't sound like that."

The bearded lady shrugs. "Late forties, early fifties."

Skelly very slowly nods. He sips some wine and puts the glass down. "So, ya see, Maia, once she told me all that, I didn't go ask Rictus nothing. Far as I could tell, there weren't a good reason anymore. We got the skinny on that Maia Gasol girly."

I don't exactly trust Ersatz. She gets along well with Rictus. Just for that, I wouldn't trust her if the word "trust" was tattooed atop her knuckles.

Unfortunately, Skelly doesn't have the same problem with trust that I do. I have come to think that he'll believe anyone as long as they'll dump a few gallons of liquor down his throat.

"Maia," Skelly says to me. "Ya… ya wanna sit here and—and have yourself a piece of… bread?"

I don't say a word. I leave him to drink Ersatz's wine.

Restless, I wander down through the tents and trailers where most of the freaks and carnies sleep. I go out to where the cars and trucks are parked like cattle herded into a loose ring. I navigate through them, and come to the tailgate of an old American pickup, which I climb on and sit. I look back at the Festival de Tordre, spread out across the field, glacier draped mountains in the background, trees encircling the area like a dark hand cupping a ball. From a distance, it's a beautiful, happy sight. If I was a visitor, I'd never guess that it's owned by a man like Rictus Fitch or that there are alcoholics, poker players, and highly skilled pickpockets working amidst and in the tents. I'd never guess that it's a dangerous place. But it is.

I wonder about Maia Gasol and if she's looking out at the place where she lives and trying to figure out her strange life, too. "Hi, Maia," I whisper, "I'm Maia. I like books, the outdoors, visiting different towns, and to talk with Skelly... you know, when he's not so drunk his stories don't make sense. What do you like?"

I continue peering fondly at the festival, the banners and flags snapping in the breeze whenever it kicks up. Atop my head, I feel my hair shift like it's reaching for the ground. I pay no attention and am caught by surprise when something warm and wet, like someone's breath, puffs against my bare feet. Rising, I glance down and there's a wild hog standing right beside the truck's bumper.

It studies me, its pig nose moving and shifting. It has a large, long, and bushy pig's body with hard straight fur that forms a ridge of brownish black down its back. I like its tusks. They're stained yellow and rise like giant teeth from its mouth, curling around its face. I've seen pictures of Medusa where she has tusks that are almost exactly the same. In those pictures, Medusa is awful looking, while the boar's face is lovely and soft, its eyes warm and intelligent. I especially enjoy seeing its hooves, which seem way too small for its body size, like it's wearing high heel shoes, which I'd like to have a pair of.

Climbing down off the truck tailgate, I scratch the boar's wedge-shaped head, causing its little tail to flap. Coils of my hair unravel and stroke the animal's long back. Clearly satisfied, it steps close to me and presses its flat, wet nose against the back of my hand like it's a large postal stamp. Then it turns and ambles away, through the jumble of cars and trucks, toward the woods.

"Thanks for coming," I call, wondering, just wondering, if Maia Gasol is good with wild animals, too.

The rest of the day is a blur, the night similar. This evening, from my cage, I search the crowd in front of me for the old woman from the night before. I want so badly to ask her questions. Because I don't trust anything Ersatz has to say, I want to know where Maia was born, who her parents were, and if her parents attempted to kill her at birth? I want to know if they considered her evil, too.

But the lady doesn't come, so nothing changes.

I barely sleep, making the night long while the morning feels short. The sun seems to break the horizon in an instant, exposing blue sky and clouds moving like icebergs from horizon to horizon.

I get up and wander toward the dining tent for food. Along the way, I pass a new carnie who doesn't go anywhere without his large German Shepard dog by his side. I've seen them working together from a distance, pulling ropes and hauling tent stakes.

When the dog sees me, though, its triangular ears go flat, and it yelps like it's been spanked before it scampers behind its master's legs to hide from me.

The carnie, who I don't really know, stops and looks at me. The three of us are frozen for a good half minute before I scratch an itch on my cheek with a tress of hair. At that, the poor, terrified animal pees all over the guy's feet. "Eh, Sampson, no!" the carnie commands with a thick British accent.

I shake my head and continue on to the tent, where I listen for Skelly's voice before I go inside and make myself a quick breakfast, and return to my trailer to read.

Later, I go for a walk. It's midday. A storm sweeps across the huge valley. I stand and watch it. Some of the cloud formations rise like snowy chimneys. In the distance, I can see Göllheim just over a series of hills. It looks small and vulnerable. Then, overhead, three American jets pass, rocketing down the broad valley.

I just started reading a book called *Huckleberry Finn* again. I've read it twice before. In it, a really funny, uneducated white boy named Huck has adventures with an escaped black slave on an American river called the Mississippi.

Whenever I read the story, I think about poor Jim, who is the slave. I know that my life in the Festival de Tordré isn't nearly as bad as his was in America, before their civil war. I'm not a slave. Slaves were worked from dawn till dark before going home to drafty houses and no food. They didn't have any control over their lives. Me, I've got my shiny trailer, and my hours of work aren't so long if I don't consider the fact that I can't ever leave the area without permission.

I wander through nearby fields, trying to lose myself to the landscape. In the distance, I can see silver flashes off the surface of the Rhine River. A ship is pushing northward, sending out a rolling, V-shaped wake behind it. If there's a gift to living the way I do, it's the travel.

I sigh and dig my hands in my pockets. Then my hair hisses harshly, and I spin about.

Skelly nods at me. "Ya been avoiding me, eh, Maia?"

"Some."

"Sorry 'bout the Bearded Lady thing yesterday. I… I don't claim to be a good man, but Ersatz, she seemed to have information that settled the mystery of Maia Gasol."

"You drink too much."

"Yeah, tha's true."

I don't say a word to him for a moment. I hear a whine in the air, turn and watch a wasp buzz about past my hair, which reaches out and brushes it. I lift a finger, and it lands softly on a knuckle. I touch its wings, look at Skelly, and say, "I still want to talk to the woman, Skelly. Is that wrong?"

He closes his eyes. "No. It's not lass."

I continue patting the wasp.

"Child, believe me, there's more to this than ya could guess. There's reasons for Rictus' overreaction yesterday, for shaking you up the way he did. There's reasons for everything."

I walk away, carrying the wasp like a tiny parrot. I stop and turn. "What are they?"

He shrugs. "How about I tell ya some other time?"

"That doesn't help me right now."

"Listen, I came to tell ya I'll go find the lady, Maia. I'll find the old woman, but I can't bring her back here, so I want ya to tell me exactly what ya wants to find out from her?"

"Just things… things about Maia Gasol."

Skelly sniffs at the air, which smells like hay.

I stand silently, thinking. I feel as if Skelly is so forgetful that I'm limited to one question. "Ask her what Maia Gasol's parents did when she was born. That's all I want to know."

"Aye." He lowers his head, raises it and frowns at me. "But I recognize the basis for your question, and it's a blow to my heart, child."

He starts to leave but stops after only a few steps. "Maia, let me be the first to say that your parent's didn't think ya was a curse, child. No, ya been believing that for way too long." He rubs his cheeks with a hand. "They loved ya with all the love they owned in their souls. And they didn't ever leave ya to die. What they're guilty of is leaving ya to be taken."

I'm not sure what he means. Distantly, I lift my finger, and the wasp takes flight. Meanwhile, Skelly shuffles away and across the fields toward the carnival. I wait till he's out of sight, then I suddenly turn and holler, "Stop! I don't get what you mean?" But, he doesn't hear me and my legs are too shaky to run after him.

8
TO STONE

I stand here, in what must be one of the most beautiful places on earth, and I wonder what Skelly meant. "They," meaning my parents, "didn't ever leave ya to die." Why would he say that, when I've heard the story of how I came to the sideshow about a thousand times? The truth about my past is as solid as stone, while my future seems enclosed by walls. I know where I'll be in five years. I know where I'll be in ten. I don't think I'll ever stop wanting to leave the Festival de Tordré, but I won't ever go. I am the Medusa child who was saved at birth by evil Rictus Fitch. I was immediately introduced to the life of a freak in a freak show. It's all I know.

I start walking and imagine myself a baby in the festival. I wonder who, if anyone, ever held me. I wonder who treated me kindly. Maybe I was simply passed from snake charmers to palm readers like something no one could get themselves to touch, like something disgusting. For all I know, Skelly was the only one who ever showed me kindness. Poor drunken Skelly.

I head for my trailer. On the way, I lean and pick up a large, dark brown stone, which I give to a shimmering lock of hair that dips down to take it. Like a child, it weighs it before winding up and whipping it so far I wonder if it'll hit the Rhine River, which must be twenty or thirty kilometers away.

I play outside my trailer, bouncing a volleyball against the side for over an hour, popping it with my hands and rigid coils of my hair so that it never touches the ground the entire time. Meanwhile, a very dark squirrel watches me from a few feet away, standing at the bottom of a tree like a referee, totally relaxed, as if fascinated by my ball bouncing talent. Done, I tell the squirrel goodbye, go into my trailer, and read different chapters in *Jaws*, which is such a frightening book that it causes the hairs on my neck to stand up.

Eventually, I clean the trailer, scrub the dirty ring from the bottom of my toilet, wash my sink, and sweep my floor. When I'm done, I organize my Medusa makeup and wash the mirror above it. But Skelly doesn't return, making me wonder if he's not drunk in a bar somewhere. It wouldn't be a shock.

Late in the afternoon, I give up on him and dress like Medusa's Daughter, which I hate, and leave my trailer for my cage.

Willem is waiting for me, sort of blocking my way.

"Excuse me, Willem," I say, trying to get by. I turn to step around him.

He steps in my way.

I go in the other direction, and he does, too.

"What?" I ask.

Snickering, Willem leers at me, a blank gaze in his blank eyes. It's sad, but he's not bright at all. Everyone in the festival says that he was a normal boy before I went about battering him for no reason when I was a child. But that's not true. I remember the way he was. I was seven and he was ten, but he could hardly speak. He was more like a parrot.

"What do you want?" I say to him sharply. I don't like Willem. I feel sorry that he's slow, but he's also got a terrible mean streak inside of him. He enjoys hurting people.

He grins widely, like a little boy looking through glass at a piece of cake. He says, "It's about something I know."

"What do you know, Willem?" I say annoyed.

He grins in his lopsided way. "That me and Atel carried Skelly back to here," he says slowly, like his tongue is numb.

"You carried Skelly from where?"

"From town. We got him good, too."

I frown. "You mean… you hurt him?"

"Yeah." He smiled. "I even knocked his head to the street."

"Why?"

"'Cause Rictus told us to."

Alarmed, I say, "Why do you listen to Rictus?"

"It's because Momma says he's the boss."

"Where is Skelly?" I ask, my voice breaking.

"He's inside his trailer is where we left him."

Fearful that I've gotten Skelly into trouble, I run down along the midway, the tents and booths a blur. Turning, I rush into the residential village, where I come to his dirty trailer, remove my glasses, and yank open the door, entering into the darkness. The floor beneath my feet is littered with bottles, some standing, others on their side. They fall down in a clatter each time I step. My eyes adjust, and I see Skelly in the back, spread out like an exhausted animal on his bunk. I say, "Skelly. Skelly?"

He turns over and his face looks horrible. "Wha, love?"

"Willem told me you're hurt."

"Did he, the creepy, slow-witted, sadistic moron? Boy nearly cracked me skull on the ground, don't ya know? Course I'm hurt."

I can't speak because of a catch in my throat. Skelly is the only family I have and he looks like he could die at any moment. Blood has dried on his face. His eyes are swollen. I say, "Why? Why did he do it?"

"Ya mean, aside from the fact he enjoyed it?"

"I guess, yeah."

"Did it 'cause I went into the police station trying to get information on the woman who came to your cage the other night."

I lean back against his dresser, which is built into the trailer. It takes me a minute to ask. "It doesn't make sense."

"What?"

"That they'd bother you there. He doesn't care about the old lady. He didn't even meet her."

"He might care."

I can't think of a singular possible reason why he would. He was mad at me for talking to her and nothing more, and I hadn't actually done that. Why would the woman be off limits to Skelly? "Why?"

"Why what?"

"Why would he care about her?"

Skelly looks up, every angle of his face an awful sight. "There are wicked things at work here, Maia Gasol. Good Mr. Fitch and your fine and wonderful guardian, Skelly, are blameworthy for most of them, too."

I think about what he has just said and ask, "Maia Gasol? Why did you call me that?"

"Because Ersatz lied to you, and I let her."

Excitement courses right through my fingertips. "Are… me and Maia related? Is that what you mean?"

"It is so. That's the truth, dolly. You're very related."

I can hardly speak. My hair is on end and reaching out for nearby objects.

Groaning and wincing, Skelly sits up higher, puts his hands on the edge of his thin mattress pad, and laughs out loud, which looks like it hurts.

"Maybe… you should rest flat," I tell him, because I worry he might topple over and cut his head on something in his trailer.

"No, I'm okay, Lassy." He feels his battered face. "Lord, Atel and Willem have got some big knuckles." He looks toward his tiny galley kitchen. "Maia, I never did speak to the woman today. Never got close. But… but that don't mean I don't probably know who she is. I figure I've got to admit to that."

"Admit to what?"

"Knowing who she is."

I blurt, "Who?"

He swallows and gurgles, like his throat is closing. "Lassy, if… if I tell you, everything changes. Everything in your bloody life changes. That's my warning. You will be crossing a line you can't ever step back from."

I don't know how to reply.

He staggers to his feet and leans against a wall of cabinets. He raises his chin, and I know that whatever he says is painfully important to my life.

"Imagine, Maia, it's fifteen years back. Everything is different. It was a totally different time. The Fesitval de Tordre has been traveling Europe for five years, but it's slowly going under, and, for reasons that have to do with being in trouble with the law in America, the owner, an American fella named Rictus Fitch, can't simply sell it and go back to the states."

"Then, as luck or bad luck would have it, one night in a bar he runs into a slimy, slick talking Irishman. Let's call this Irishman, Paddy. Paddy is looking to make his way. Paddy is looking to be somebody more than he was where he grew up. Paddy has ideas about how to run a large enterprise. He proceeds to befriend this unlikeable Rictus fella. Takes months to gain his trust, but when he does, Paddy uses everything he's learned to blackmail him, to threaten him with contacting the American police if he doesn't get half ownership of the Festival de Tordré right up front. 'Right now!' he told him."

"Rictus is trapped with nothing but a few bad choices. He could've risked killing the Paddy, which ain't something he was above doing. Then again, he'd be wanted on two continents. He could've ignored the Paddy's threats. Or he could sign."

"Rictus says, 'Don't turn your back on me, Paddy. Don't trust a single one of my intentions. I don't forgive or forget thieves.'"

"'Fine. I don't expect ya to.'"

"And Rictus, he folds the knife closed and signs half of the Festival de Tordré, over to the slimy Irishman."

"Soon as the Paddy becomes half owner, he goes about improving the show's cash flow. He's got big plans and is a ruthless bloke. Whereas Rictus dabbled in pickpockets, the Paddy floods the place with them. Whereas Rictus has a few gambling tables, the Paddy dedicates three big tents, placing them behind main attractions and freak show houses along the midway and such. Whereas Rictus had a few scams, the Paddy makes it a funhouse of such things. And quick as you want, Maia, the money problems go away. And to the Paddy, it doesn't even seem like Rictus much cares he gave up partial ownership with the kind of money they got coming in."

"But, over a few years, ya see, Rictus and Paddy figure they got to make improvements on The Festival de Tordré's sorry sideshow acts. They're ratty and poor and even that group of sorrowful losers and crummy freaks is leaving left and right. Worse, they're drawing fewer actual visitors than the gambling tables. I mean, if there ain't no reason for anybody to come to the sideshow, but American servicemen are still flooding the place, law enforcement might very well get suspicious of the activities taking place."

"So Rictus and this Paddy fella start searching for better freaks. And that ain't difficult in Europe. You remember the Human Knob's poor head?"

"Yeah," I tell him softly.

"Well, that sort of disfigurement was easy to find after the war. But Rictus and the Paddy want the real thing. They want the amazing."

"A few months into their search, they're in Germany when they hear rumors about a child, the daughter of an American Air Force pilot, who could move her hair to and yon and wherever she wants. Now they'd heard other rumors about other freaks, all of which had ended up to be nothing. There was the bat boy in France. Little ball buster was just a kid with strange ears. In Italy, there was the human ant, but she was just your typical midget. There was a lizard man in Spain who had nothing but dry skin, close set eyes and overgrown fingernails."

"See, none of them was astounding. None of them could move their hair. Ain't that an unusual talent? Except, there's a problem. Her parents, who love her dearly, are worried 'bout the way people will treat her, so they don't talk up the details of her strangeness. They try to keep it secret."

"Course, money loosens lips, and Rictus and the Paddy are loosening 'em all around Germany... A lieutenant and his wife say they've seen this girl move her hair at their daughter's birthday party. In school, a teacher watches her reach for pencils with them crazy locks. People talk, Maia... And the Paddy and Rictus knew who to talk to back, like an air base pediatrician who hates his job. The guy doesn't feel no conflict of interest in discussing his patients. The guy was a worst sot than me and at least two to three hundred times more vain."

"Picture this very handsome, very self-absorbed doctor and these two untrustworthy grifters who went in the door and started up a conversation with him. Eventually, he says, 'So, ya two own a freak show? God, that must be a hoot.'"

"Rictus tells him, 'Let me buy you a few more rounds, fella. And, yup, we own a sideshow and we're looking for freaks and not a bunch of war wounded. We're looking for the real thing. Ya got any ideas on it?'"

"'Freaks? Well, Christ, I got a little fella with seven fingers on one hand, two thumbs and two pointers. It's odd.' He knocks back a glass of booze. 'I seen a little boy in town here with a square foot. We call it club foot, but I haven't ever seen such a square foot before in my professional career. Looks like he's part horse.' He paused and dabbled with his nice hair. He thought for a minute, drank some more, then he said to the two grifters, 'Okay. Here's something. It's sort of a secret, but I got a real winner for you. Weirdest thing I ever saw.'"

"What?'

"What'cha paying?"

"Rictus told him, 'Could be a heart stopping amount.'"

Skelly pauses and looks at me. His beaten up face gives him a sad, faraway look. No matter, I'm beginning to see that he isn't who he has presented himself to be.

"The doctor," Skelly continues, "he leaned forward and answered, 'This little girl on base, she's got living hair. It's freakish. Like an octopus. I'm telling you, I stick a tongue suppressor in her mouth to check her tonsils, and a lock wraps tight as hell around my wrist. It's... it's doggone unsettling.'"

"Rictus asked, 'Is she an American's child or the child of a local who works on base?'"

"Airman's."

"What's her last name?"

"Confidential. I can't... you know... speak it aloud. I'm legally bound."

"Well, Herr Doctor, why don't ya write it on a piece of paper and we'll buy the information?"

"The doctor, he looked at him, Maia, and you could tell what the answer was. He wrote it down, and the three of them headed outside to do business. They circled around toward the back of the building, and the tipsy, idiot doctor blurted, 'Ah, hell, I'll just say it. Her name's Gasol. That's her last name. Her first name's Maia."

"'Thanks,' Rictus told the man, but it wasn't in a nice way. The doctor, who has to be helped along by the Paddy and Rictus, blabbered, 'Ya ever heard of a male model, boys?'"

"'No,' the Paddy said back to him."

"It's a man who's so handsome he's paid to pose in magazines, showing off suits and blazers and the like. You think I could do something like that? I always wondered, 'cause, believe me, I feel like I've wasted my life in medicine."

"Rictus reached into his coat pocket, and said, 'You won't be wasting it anymore, doc, I promise.' In a blur, a knife lashes the man's stomach."

"'What tha hell?' the Paddy screamed, because he hadn't planned on hurting no one. Mouth open, the Paddy, goes, 'Why? Why'd ya do it?'"

"Rictus told him, 'We couldn't grab the child and leave this bone cutter to roll on us. It wouldn't be smart. We're covering bases.'"

"But the Paddy, he don't want nothing of it. 'Ya… ya just made us murderers.'"

"Wiping the blade, Rictus just sneered at him in that way he does when he feels like he's got ya beat. He said, 'Can't believe you're getting squeamish. I've never seen you experience a moment's remorse in all these years. Not a moment's.' He turned and pointed threateningly. 'I was weak when ya took part of the festival from me, but I'm not weak anymore. Murder is the tie that binds us. Who can say which one of us did this terrible thing? Our fingerprints are all over that bar. And we didn't exactly try and hide our faces. Besides, as I recall it, killing this idiot was your idea… or at least that's what I'll tell the police." He stopped and looked at the doctor on the ground. 'Now, I'll go get the car. We'll throw the good doctor in the trunk and drop him outside of town.'"

There's absolute silence. We are back in the moment facing off. I look at Skelly. He looks at me. He rubs at the dried blood on his face.

I fiddle with the edge of my glasses. The other hand plays with the rough, loose fabric of my burlap dress. I speak very softly, like I'm trying to swallow back my request. "Skelly, tell me that wasn't you."

Skelly blinks and trembles spastically. "Took… took a week for us to grab the kid. I followed her everywhere, too, whenever she was off base. Her parents even brought her to the festival, where they wandered about enjoying the games. Was when she was visiting a downtown grocery off base with her nurse or nanny, whatever ya like to call them, that I finally got her. Back then, children stayed outside with all the other youngins while adults went in to stores to shop. Your nanny being German, she did the same thing, and when she came outside from buying groceries, she found that you was gone."

I can't speak. I can't say a word. It's strange to learn in an instant that your life was stolen from you, that everything you could've been is gone and everything you are didn't have to be.

"Worse," Skelly tells me, "I recognized your old nanny all these years later. I could see it in her eyes. I believe we ruined her life nearly as much as we ruined the lives of your parents."

I shake my head, which feels surrounded by storm clouds.

"Maia, I led ya away from your friends, taped your mouth, and settled ya inta the same trunk your doctor took a ride in the week before." He swallowed. "Ya was only four, but ya kicked and screamed and that hair like to snap my wrists."

I tell him, "Stop talking.'"

He hesitates before saying, "For a month, Rictus kept ya in the very trailer you're in now, and it wasn't too long before ya began to see him as your guardian. I suppose ya had to. Winter was coming, and like every year we turned and headed south to the Mediterranean Sea. We was in Southern Italy when Rictus booked us passage across the Ionian Sea to Greece. That's where he thought up all the hokey Medusa tripe."

I'm shaking my head, sickened by what I'm hearing and shocked that I can't remember any of it. Nothing. My old life with real parents is a blank, wiped away like it never was.

"Ya gave up who ya were pretty quickly. I was sort of shocked. But, I guess kids are flexible and can become whatever they need to be to survive." He stops, and breathes for a minute before saying, "And, Maia, your kidnapping, dear, it was huge news. Your ma and dad and nanny, they was obviously devastated by their loss. The papers ran their stories for weeks. It broke my heart. It did. Swiping ya ate a hole in me. I wanted to take ya back. I did, but Rictus wouldn't allow for it. I begged him. I was so melancholy and disgusted with meself. I was nearly as lost as your parents. I was lost in every way. Signed over my half of the festival to Rictus, because I hated it so much. I didn't even care no more. What's money when ya got a hole the size of the Nile River running right through your soul?"

I want to slap Skelly. I have no words to describe my feelings. My identity, who I am, feels lost. I feel as if I've suddenly been enclosed in darkness, like the ground and sky have gone oil-black and I might suddenly rise up into it and choke.

I'm a lie.

I've always been a lie. I sway, nearly getting sick.

Skelly leans forward, holding his battered guts with a hand. He coughs, which makes his face go white as china. "Maia..." he grumbles, "believe me. What I done to ya ruined me. I had meself a breakdown in Greece. Couldn't stand meself and the thing that I done to ya."

I look into his puddling, puffy eyes. My hair rubs together like hundreds of tiny violins. "I know the feeling, Skelly. I've hated myself, too, what with worrying I was a monster." I want to strike him, to hurt him for stealing me from my parents, for making me a sideshow act.

"Maia, a man can cheat folks of money, but money isn't warm, don't smile, and don't breathe. I'm not a bloke who can stab pediatricians or take kids from their families and not lose my mind for doing it."

"Good," I hiss, wiping away tears.

"But… Maia, over tha years, I've tried hard to make it up to ya. I tried to protect ya from Rictus and the other festival folk. I cared for ya like ya was my own." He gently puts a trembling hand on my shoulder. "I tried to be like a surrogate parent."

Pulling away, I scream, "Don't touch me! Don't!"

"Maia," he groans as I push the door open.

Rushing down the steps, I nearly tumble into Horst, who is accompanied by Rictus.

"What have we here, Horst?" Rictus asks as he marches forward. "Our little monster appears to have seen a ghost." He grabs my arm and yanks me close, causing my elbow to hurt and making me wish my arms were as strong as my hair. "What did he say to you, Maia? What did he say?"

"Nothing," I lie, suddenly more frightened of Rictus than ever before.

Horst laughs.

"Shut up, Horst," Rictus snarls.

Behind me, I hear Skelly's trailer door swing open.

Rictus grins. "Dicussing old times, were we Skelly?"

"No." He stumbles from his trailer. "Just trying to recover from the working over your boys gave me."

Horst snickers again.

Rictus is holding his walking stick, gripping it so tightly his knuckles are white with little wreaths of red around them. "Maia, my little gorgon monster of The Festival de Tordré, scurry back to your cage and do the evening show like a good little pet. Skelly and I must talk."

"No," I say softly.

"No!" Rictus barks, glancing around him and digging the tip of his stick into the dirt. "You'll get in your proper place, or I'll make you."

I say, "I don't want to be Medusa's Daughter anymore."

He leans forward, ignoring my hair. His eyes practically spit acid. "Maia, as I said earlier today, I've loved you like a father, but fathers have their limits, and you're walking the edge of mine. Bear in mind, what's love but dominance and its counterpart fear, Maia? It's always the one with the other. Consider it my place to dominate and yours to fear. In that way, don't we love one another deeply?"

Before I can stop myself, I rasp, "Go away, Rictus."

The back of his hand hits me so hard I stagger backwards, dropping my Medusa glasses to the ground. Suddenly, my nerve is shaken, my courage on the verge of crumbling completely or rising beyond the fear Rictus has imprinted so deeply onto my soul.

I have no idea which way it will go.

"Rictus!" Skelly says, stumbling over to help me.

But I don't want his help. I move away from him. Everything he's ever done is a either a lie or based on guilt.

Noting my reaction, Rictus bangs the tip of his walking stick to the ground again. "So you told her everything, didn't you, Skelly? When you saw that old crone, your guilt flared up, didn't it?"

Furious, I say to Rictus, "You're a liar. You've lied to me. You didn't find me on a rock."

He smiles and points the tip of his walking stick at me.

"Maia, without me, you would've been nothing." He steps closer. "Without me, you're the impoverished daughter of an American Air Force officer, a girl doomed to die from depression, drink, or a drug overdose. No one can love you. It's taken me years to stomach your presence. I made you and you embraced what you became, the predator, the creature. You're Medusa's Daughter, and if you aren't, then you're just an undereducated freak who'll be rejected by society and studied by scientists."

I don't move. The people around me don't make a sound, either. He thinks I'm bothered by his speech, but I'm not.

Skelly says, "Stop it, Rictus!"

Horst slams Skelly, who looks like a pummeled scarecrow, against the side of his trailer.

Rictus turns menacingly and stares at me. "Horst, my friend Skelly, my business partner, has come to the end of his useful life. What do you think? Should I kill him, Maia? For eleven long years, I've carried him. He's a drunk. He's unreliable and uncreative. Worse, he's joyless."

I can feel my heart beating so that it sounds like a series of muffled strikes against the back of my tongue.

"Teach him, Horst," Rictus says.

Horst cocks a fist back.

But I move in front of Skelly, protecting him.

"Move away, lassy," Skelly says to me.

Horst roars, "Don't think I wouldn't enjoy hitting you, Maia!"

"Oh, my!" Rictus howls joyfully. "She's so brave, isn't she Horst. Oh, so brave. Ah, well, might as well teach her, too!"

I don't budge. I'm not scared of Horst, not since the day I injured his arm when I was nine or ten. But he outweighs me by about two hundred pounds, so I study him and try to figure out what to do if he comes after me. Then, before I come to a conclusion, my hair shoots out at Horst's fist, entwining his entire forearm to the elbow.

It's a wonderful sensation to have such a hateful man in my control. I tighten the coils so that Horst's eyes seem to bulge painfully in their sockets. Shifting my attention, I say to Skelly, "Leave!" I find it hard to protect him after what he's just told me. "Go," I order Skelly again, just as I notice the sound of a fox vomiting up a rabbit or a bird. I glance back at Horst and am horrified to see that it's not a fox at all. I'm choking him. His face is red, his mouth trembling like he's been locked in a walk-in freezer. Horrified, by what's happening, I throw him to the ground, and he topples like a marionette when the strings are cut.

Rictus watches coldly. "Am I next, Maia," he says mockingly.

I spin to look at him. I hiss like some kind of strange reptile. The bizzare sound resonates in my throat, and I'm embarrassed for making it. At the moment, I seem more monster than girl. Then again, who is to blame for that? Who has stated and stated that I'm the child of gorgons? None other than Rictus Fitch.

Like a big cat, I show him my teeth.

He snickers anxiously at me, his long straight hair brushing his round shoulders and the top of his fancy ringmaster jacket. He grips his walking stick in the middle then gives it a solid yank at the top, withdrawing a long blade, a sword. "Girl, you come over here and I'll split that foul head. I won't think twice."

I don't wait for him to get into a defensive stance. My hair, like a seething, clicking mass of reptiles and raptors, lunges and entangles Rictus. He swings the sword at me, but I avoid it.

My hair lashes around his arms, and he tries to pull away. He attempts to drive the blade into me, but I control him, and I can see how he suddenly realizes that. The sound in my throat becomes bloodcurdling.

Desperate, he says, "I'm n… n… not scared of you, Maia. You're a… a… a pet, completely submissive."

I screech, sounding like a hawk gliding toward an animal. I can feel myself fading away, my personality replaced by something less human.

Rictus says, "You'll die a nobody."

I pull him closer. He smiles like he's trying to convince me he's harmless.

We lock eyes.

I smile back.

Seconds pass. Then he starts to hurt. He bellows but can't unlock his gaze from mine. I can see the sideshow folks approaching, curious at the noise. Confused, I pull away from Rictus, who stumbles backwards and covers his eyes with the hand that had been entangled in my hair. The other arm is useless and appears to be swaying heavily at his side. Its coloration has changed to grayish brown, like wet German rocks.

Absorbed by instinct, I rush Rictus, slamming into him. He stumbles backward over one of Skelly's empty bottles and falls so that his hand, turned to stone, strikes the rocky ground, breaking.

In pain, he curses.

I hiss, "Look into my eyes, Rictus."

But he keeps his head turned and his eyes covered. He whimpers, "How? How can this be? You can't do this, it was a story, a joke."

"But it's not, and you made it so," I answer. It doesn't sound like me at all. Recognizing that, I feel a wind, like a cold breeze from a glacier or off a glacial river, rush against my shoulders. I shake my head wildly, lower to a knee, and return.

"Maia," Skelly says over Rictus' babbling.

Covering my eyes, I say, "My glasses, Skelly. I need them. They're somewhere on the ground."

I can hear him searching about before he finds them in the dirt. I put them on and open my eyes to see Horst who has fallen to his knees. It's likely that his Nazi brain is whirling as he calculates what to do without the help of Rictus.

"We needs a car, lassy," Skelly says, ignoring everyone around us.

I nod but don't take my eyes off of Horst, who, despite his hopeless stupidity and inability to think for himself, remains towering and dangerous. He looks at me, a girl with a slight build, skinny arms, and spindly legs. He takes a deep breath, stands, and walks slowly away like he's stared down the bony gullet of one of those Alaskan grizzly bears with their matted fur, claws like ice hooks, and big yellow teeth that are thick and sharp as infectious spear points.

"He'll come out of that trance, Maia, and eventually fetch Atel and Willem, that's for sure," Skelly says. "Meaning, dear, that me and ya gotta shove off."

I look at the people I've worked with for as long as I can remember. I look at Skelly's trailer and think of my own with my book collection and the few things that I own, a broken music box from Portugal, some clothes that I think are nice, a bracelet I never get to wear accept in the mornings. But why do I need any of it any more? Rictus was right. I am a gorgon. I have turned, or started to turn, a man to stone.

Skelly steps over Rictus. Glowering down at the man, he studies the broken arm, before saying, "Rictus, me dear business partner, I need your keys."

His stone arm propped on a leg, Rictus sits up and stares at us silently.

Skelly places a foot against his chest, pushing him back to the ground. "Ya gonna give them to me, bloke, or do I got to go fish for them?"

Rictus' eyes are vacant, his irises practically wobbling. He swallows and says, "I was nice to you," in a high nervous voice. "I kept you on even though you were a… drunk."

"I made ya rich," Skelly tells him, "and I never saw a penny." He sticks out his hand. "The keys?"

"Maia," Rictus mutters, "I was like a father to you. I cared for you, gave you your own trailer, made you the star."

I don't reply.

Foot still on Rictus, Skelly leans down and rifles his coat, locating the keys. "Thanks, Ricky from Detroit."

I look over and ask, "His name is Ricky?"

Skelly nods. "Oh, yeah, deary. Real name's Ricky Marion Fitch. Little Ricky, who burned down his parents home when he was six, whose drunken dad didn't work and whose mother got carted away to an insane asylum for being terrified of the man who lived in the water pipes under her sinks. Isn't that so, Ricky?"

Rictus, who seems like he's about to fall asleep says, "You... you stupid Mick... You got no right to tell her or anyone that stuff."

"Seems to me, Ricky, Maia has every right in the world to know about the man who ruined her life."

"Who do you mean, me or you, Skelly?"

Skelly nods. "Could be either one of us, it's true. But I'm gonna make up for it now. I'm gonna get her away from you."

Then Skelly and I run along the backside of the midway, past the fortune teller's display, sword swallower's pavilion, and the gambling caravans. We rush into the forest of trailers and sleeping tents. Skelly, though, suddenly stops cold. "Forgot something. Wait right here, dear," he says, and runs back toward the midway.

Time passes. A minute, five, ten, I can't tell. Then he returns, limping from the beating he took earlier and carrying a bag.

He says to me, "Had the keys to the safe, love, so I thought I should use it."

I want to tell him not to call me love anymore.

"I figure Rictus owes me and ya about ten years of back payments. More than that, you're gonna need cash to give ya a fresh start and a chance." He pushes me forward, and we arrive at the field where the cars and automobiles are parked chaotically. Skelly searches around for a few moments before he finds Rictus's favorite car. We both get in, his face as angular and swollen as a diamond.

Me, I have no energy. I have no strength. I feel ruined, like I could ooze into the seat and never raise myself off of it.

Shutting his door, Skelly starts the engine. He slides the car into gear, and we bump across the field till we come to the paved road, where he crawls out onto the thoroughfare. Hitting the gas, he wipes at the dried blood beneath his nose as the festival and parked cars and visitors and gamblers fall away behind us.

It unsettles me to realize that every kilometer we drive takes me farther and farther from the world of dwarfs, musclemen, illusionists, bearded ladies, and fortune tellers. It is the world I've known for all of my life, or at least the life I remember, and I'm not sure I'll do well in the normal world, in a regular bedroom that doesn't hook to a truck or in a school that forces students to sit for hours learning how to put numbers together.

A few years ago, I read a magazine story about a girl named Patty Hearst, who was the famous rich daughter of a famous rich newspaper family who got kidnapped by violent hippies. Like me, she began to think that she belonged with her hippie group in the same way I joined Rictus' sideshow and became their freak. We were both gullible.

"What's wrong?" Skelly asks.

Head down, I can't help but think he's stupid for wondering. When I speak, I try not to sound mean. "Did you see what I did? I'm dangerous, Skelly."

He glances at me from the corner of his eye. "Aye, very dangerous, child. Ya're dangerous to dangerous people. Tell me,

Maia, if good destroys evil, does good remain good? I think it does. That's what I think."

"I don't know what you mean," I tell him.

He nods. "I mean that ya are good and that Rictus is evil. And the fact that ya destroyed someone who's evil doesn't suddenly make ya evil."

"What does it make me?" I ask sarcastically.

"I think it makes ya still good, child."

"But I'm not safe to be around."

"I'm around ya. Ya are fine."

"You should leave me."

He lowers his hand to the seat. "I ain't leaving ya till I know you're on your way to somewhere better."

I don't want to hear him act like he cares. "Where's that?" I ask softly.

"I been thinking, Maia. It's time ya leave Europe. I'm sending ya back to tha States so that ya can catch up to your parents. Ya needs to start again. And Ersatz says Köln is the place to go. She says that more than a few ship captains are happy to take money for carrying human cargo over the Atlantic."

"I don't trust, Ersatz."

He shrugs. "She wants to leave Rictus just like ya did."

"She thinks I ruined Willems' life."

"Naw, she don't. Not really. She knows it ain't true."

We travel slowly north through the darkness, pass medieval towns, and others that were destroyed by Allied bombs during World War II. As we go, I think over my scuffle with Rictus. I want to find an easily explained reason for what I did to him, something that will assure me I'm not a gorgon and just a girl stressed enough to turn flesh and bone to stone.

Exhausted, I eventually close my eyes and fall to sleep, where I have a nightmare. I dream of Rictus, which is always bad.

He's inside a carnival tent, light catching his face and highlighting the fat hairs curling on his snout. Rictus looks like the large man-pig named Napoleon from *Animal Farm*. Napoleon, who ruled the farm by turning animals against one another. He chased away his competition, and intimidated others with his small army of mean dogs. He ruled with an iron fist. Napoleon was awful, and Rictus is Napoleon and Napoleon is Rictus. They're both pigs.

I see Rictus the pig annoying snakes with a walking stick. He pushes at their coiled bodies with a hoofed hand, and they hiss at him furiously. He belittles each, kicks at them all, spits into their slanted eyes till, furious, they strike, springing forward at him.

Blackness.

I'm passing down a river that looks like a lava flow of molten gold. Its gentle ripples appear polished to a perfect sheen. Green banks rush softly by. A few leafy trees bend down to drag a branch in the water. I think of *Huckleberry Finn* and the black man named Tom who were afloat on the Mississippi, searching for a new home. They were travelers forced from their communities, just like me. In fact, me and Skelly both are searching for a new and safe place. I lean and dip my foot into the water so that my guilt can fade and my pain ease, so that I can wash the dirt of my life away.

I startle awake.

Skelly has stopped the car. It's still dark out. He's trying to clean his battered face in the rearview mirror even though his hands are trembling.

I ask, "What's wrong?" but I don't say it nicely.

He explains to me, "I got to go in this here store to buy me something to handle me alcohol shakes, so I'm just trying to clean up a little."

I watch his hands. "What are alcohol shakes?"

"When a person's so used to drinking alcohol, their body begins to tremble if they don't get it. It's on account of me being an alcoholic."

I nod, disgusted.

"Sorry, Maia, but I can hardly drive like this. Besides, we needs some directions." He gets out and goes into the small store.

While he's gone, my hair explodes forward and punches all of the buttons in the car, which seems funny enough to make me smile. "Stop," I tell it, but I really don't want it to. I just want to feel better and more hopeful.

When Skelly returns, he's actually carrying a china coffee cup. Before speaking, he gulps at least half of it down. Wiping his mouth, he says, "We're outside Köln. Ersatz says we should drive into the wee city and look to get us a room above a brew house called Das Fischbein, or The Whalebone. It's by the international piers. Says that all sorts of sailors make the place their home away from home while their ship's getting loaded and unloaded. She thinks we can find us a boat overseas there."

"Did you steal that cup?" I ask, harshly, as I hadn't heard a word he'd said.

He shakes his head. "No, I bought it from the lady since she didn't have no throw away cup or nothing."

I look out the window as he drinks the remainder of his coffee in a few big swallows. Some of it spills on his stubbly chin and grimy shirt. Finished, he starts the car and everything comes to life at once. The radio blasts, the heater roars to life, and the windshield wipers wonk back and forth. It's pretty funny to me but almost gives Skelly a heart attack. Confused, he fumbles to turn everything off. Meanwhile, my hair moves about delicately, like an innocent child.

It takes a few hours to find the piers and Das Fischbein. The two of us park the car and wander through a quiet street to the inn, where, it turns out, even dressed as Medusa's Daughter, I'm not so out of place. It's early in the morning, but the place still has customers seated like zombies or swaying to and fro like shrubs bobbing in a rowboat. At the bar, which is shaped like an oval in the center of the room, men and ladies stare like they're looking ten miles into the distance, which they aren't. Also, most of them are commenting in different languages, but no one's listening. I figure it's because they've been drinking, which I hate. I hate drinking for what it does to people.

Skelly goes straight to the bar, situates himself between two women with yellow, knotted up hair, and orders a big drink of something. Feeling stupid, I stand behind him as he throws it down his throat. Done, he goes about getting us a room upstairs.

"Nein," the man says in a thick German accent, pointing at me. "Not with da girl."

"She's me daughter," Skelly lies.

The man at the bar leans and asks me, "You are his daughter, fräulein?" Fräulein, by the way, means young woman.

"Ja," I tell him, meaning yes.

He looks at me. "Can you take the glasses off, fräulein?"

"Nein," I say. "I have eye problems."

Skelly says, "Bloody bad eyes, yup."

The bartender nods.

9

DAS
FISCHBEIN

Upstairs, we open the door to a room with a bed and a couch. "Take the bed, lassy," Skelly says.

Matter of factly, I reply, "You're too tall for the couch."

"That ain't exactly so. Now, you go on and take the bed like a good girl and I'll claim the couch, which is what I'm itching for anyway. It's got a nice curve to it."

"The springs are bad," I say. But because I'm mad at him and feeling exhausted, I accept his offer and hope he'll be uncomfortable. I get into bed still wearing my Medusa suit.

Embarrassed, Skelly says to me, "I think I'm going to go down and look to meet a ship captain or two."

"And to drink?" I ask harshly.

His head lowers so that he can't meet my eyes, which have glasses covering them. "Aye, dolly, and drink."

When he's gone, I stare at the ceiling. I feel like I've got too much inside my head. As of the afternoon before, I am Maia

Gasol, the child of normal, loving American parents. Due to that, I can now say for sure that I am not related to the mythological gorgons, meaning my hair is my own strange curse separate from Medusa's. But in my life, I continually move sideways or backwards, never forwards. For instance, I can't get over what my eyes did.

It's frustrating.

My hair curls up beside me like a raccoon I slept with back when Rictus chained me to the frame of my trailer. I hold a part of it in my hand and go to sleep in sheets that smell like cigarettes and dirty socks.

I don't wake when Skelly returns.

In the morning, he's up before I am, and looking better, like his face is less swollen, his teeth even seem straighter, while his bruises have softened. He gargles with water from the sink in the room, wipes it through his hair, and says, "I'm heading out to buy us both some travel clothes."

"Travel clothes?" I ask, blinking at him.

"Ya can't wear that Medusa garb for the next month, child."

"Did you meet a captain or something?"

"Nope. I didn't, love. But I will. I'm going to, dolly." He steps forward, bends, and takes the bag of money he'd swiped out of Rictus' safe, then he leaves.

I get up and, wearing my glasses, I wash in the sink then go to use the bathroom down the hall, except I have to stand in a line for fifteen minutes because three people are ahead of me. All of them seem annoyed that I won't show my eyes. When I'm done, I return and sit on the couch. I can't stand the smell of the bed anymore. Also, I don't have anything to read, so I look out the window at the adjacent wall that has ancient bullet scars running up and down it like a child scribbled on it with a machine gun. I figure the damage is from World War II, back when Horst was a Nazi.

Soon enough, Skelly's back. He's been gone for less than an hour, but he's carrying numerous bags. He shuts the door and looks at me oddly.

"What?" I ask. I don't want to play games with him anymore.

He rubs his eyes. "Well, I… I just a few minutes ago pulled out some of the money I took from Rictus' safe. I was buying your clothes, see, and I needed a few small bills. Well, I couldn't find them. I didn't have any small bills is what I mean." He stops and grins. "Maia, I believe I stopped counting the money in this here duffel when I got over seventy thousand dollars, US."

I stand. "Is that a lot?"

"A small fortune. Christ, who'd ever guess that Rictus had that kind of coin? He's always claiming to be broke? Honey, ya carry this with ya when ya arrive in the States, and ya can buy a good life for yourself with or without a family."

"Except, it's not mine."

"Maia, ya earned this and more. Ya was on display. Ya did two shows a night and shows all weekend till midnight. Please. This is yours."

"It's yours, too, then."

He puts my new clothes on the sofa beside me. "I'll only take what I need. Now, try some of these on when ya wants."

Before noon, Skelly gets dressed in his own new set of clothes and goes down to drink alongside captains and first mates. He intends to ask them about my passage to America.

I tell him I'm going to search for an English novel to read.

"Just check in every hour or so, dear. Cause I plan on getting ya passage by this afternoon."

Once, I found a fashion magazine that had a quote on the cover. It said, Clothes make the woman! Now, I sort of wonder if it's true, because I do feel new and more like a girl. I'm even wearing perfume for the first time, which is amazing and causes me to smell like a flower, a smell that's better than just skin and sweat and hay. Also, my shirt is soft and flowy with a nice print that is girlish, while my pants fit my hips so that I feel attractive even if I might not be. Best of all, I don't feel evil. I don't feel like Medusa's Daughter.

I walk uphill and away from the busy docks, where rusty cranes the size of buildings and shaped like gargantuan prehistoric birds pecking at the ground hoist battered metal containers off of ship decks. I know. I can see them past the wall near my window.

The containers make loud noises as they slam and bang. The sound echoes throughout the area, but it is falling away now, just like the sound of forklifts and conveyor belts rumbling and growling loudly. I leave behind old and new warehouses that look big enough to hold blimps and ferries and anything anyone can possibly build. And, as I go, the town changes.

People are everywhere, strolling in very proper business suits with big collars. Others wear work pants and shirts that make them look like they'll spend the day down at the docks. Some of those men carry beers in their hands. Others carry pails or cloth wrapped around sandwiches or bratwursts.

I go into various magazine stores and other places that seem likely to have books by British or American writers, but I don't find any. I keep walking because I like the way I feel. I think boys are looking at me, which they've never done before except when they're disgusted by what they see. Maybe it's my new sunglasses, a fancy, white pair that Skelly bought that morning.

Feeling good, I go into a pastry shop and get a large piece of kuchen, which is German for cake, and eat it as I go. It's chocolate and feels so perfect in my stomach, too. To eat cake and be free and feel like I'm beautiful all at the same time makes me smile. I smile so wide I embarrass myself and look straight down at the sidewalk in front of me. But trying not to be seen causes me to giggle. It's just so nice to feel nice. There's no way to explain it.

I look up and there's a bookshop in front of me. I go in and wander around looking for books written in English, which I find in the back. I pick up something called *Conan the Barbarian*, but I really don't want to read a story about a barbarian guy who cuts other people up with a sword, so I put it down. I look around some more, and my eyes are drawn to a book about the ocean called *The Old Man and the Sea*.

I pick it up and read that it's by Ernest Hemmingway, who is famous for being a writer and for watching the bull fights in Spain. That causes me to worry that his story might be about bullfighting, but it doesn't seem like it since it takes place on an island called Cuba, where I don't think bulls live.

I take the book to the counter and the man mutters the price in German marks. Nodding, I reach into a pocket to get some. I look down and my glasses slide off of my nose and clatter on the counter. Shocked, I look up at the cashier guy, who stares back at me. We stop. I can't move for fear I'm turning him partially to stone.

He doesn't move either, until he says, "Fraulein?" I can tell he wants to know if I'm okay.

Surprised he's not frozen for ever like a sculpture, I pick up my glasses and put them on. "Mir geht es gut?" I tell him, which is German for I am fine.

He nods.

I buy the book and leave, wondering why my eyes hadn't hurt the man when Rictus' arm had frozen to stone. I don't understand the way my body works. None of it makes any sense.

When I return to the wharfs and docks, a ship is slowly pulling away from a pier, its smoke stack puffing dark streaks high into the clean blue air above, where seagulls are zipping in and out of it, riding a strong wind that I don't even feel.

I turn the corner by Das Fischbein, and Skelly is out front wandering in circles. When he sees me, he smiles. He's clearly drunk, which is annoying. Rushing up, he says, "Maia, got ya passage on a boat, but we gotta hurry."

I freeze. I guess I hadn't really expected it to happen so fast.

"It leaves in about twenty minutes, so ya gotta get a move on."

"So... soon?"

"Sooner the better."

I swallow. "Are you coming with me?"

He shakes his head. "Girly, ya don't want me, and ya shouldn't. I'm a drunk, fit for a jail cell, a barstool, or a ditch, in that order."

I don't like to hear him say that about himself. My hands rub up and down on the spine of my book. I think about arriving in a new country all alone and weighted by my issues. I say, "I don't know if I can do it."

"Aye, ya can, love. Ya can do anything ya want."

But I'm not sure it's true. I want to ask him to come, but I can't. I can't ask him for a favor.

His breath smells like the bristle-end of a toilet brush. "Now, hurry up to the room and fetch your new clothes. Then, me and ya are gonna go visit Templeton Sweeny, captain of the Sunderland Traveler. We's both Catholic boys from Belfast, which means we're in a tight club. So he's doing me a favor on this one. Says he'll personally see to your safety."

"Hurry," he tells me.

I stumble quickly away and through Das Fischbein's front doors, alongside the bar, and upstairs. Opening the door to our room, I find that Skelly has packed my clothes in two old suitcases he'd bought the day before. I drop my book in one and refasten it tightly.

I lower my head, leave, and bang the suitcase down the steps. At the bottom, though, someone stands in my way and refuses to move. I look up and my knees go weak.

Atel.

He's standing between the door and the wall picking his teeth clean with a pocket knife. He points the knife tip in my direction. "Medusa. Did you really think you'd get away? Let me give you some advice. You should never trust a rummy. Skelly listened to Ersatz. How stupid is that?"

I am not the least bit surprised Ersatz gave us up. I still can't believe that Skelly trusted her. "Where's Skelly?"

"Skelly? Oh, well Horst and Willem have him in the pathway between pallets, a block up the street by the docks. Willem wants to beat him senseless, but we've told him not to, not yet. That's up to you."

Atel holds out an arm indicating that I should walk in front of him. "Let us go have a talk."

Feeling helpless, I lift my suitcases and start walking. As I pass his shoulder, my hair hisses so loudly that the bartender and a man who appears to have fainted against the counter look up at Atel and me wondering where the noise is coming from.

Outside, I adjust my glasses while my hair shifts and corkscrews on my head like a raccoon itching to leap into Atel's face and tear off his handlebar mustache and stupid looking hat. Atel seems to realize this and steps back a bit so as not to be within grabbing distance.

As I go, the big suitcase gets heavy, so I drag it along, across the road and past a few sailors walking by. I look at them for help, but they hardly notice I'm even there. Ahead, there's a mountain of crates stacked atop one another. Deep in the shadows between them, I can see figures moving about. I go in, my eyes taking a second to adjust.

Horst stands a few feet away holding the barrel of a pistol casually against Skelly. "Well look who we have found. Medusa's Daughter. And she looks so lovely."

"New clothes," Atel comments.

Horst says, "Medusa, you see, you can't ever get away from us. It's hopeless."

Willem says, "Do we get to hurt them now? I just want to."

"Not her, just Skelly. He will not be coming home, so feel free to have a little fun with him."

Willem laughs. "You mean anything?"

"As much as you like... unless our dear Medusa wants to cooperate."

I hate these men. They are Rictus' secret police. They are the intimidating foot soldiers of Rictus' sideshow world. They make threats and deliver on them, scaring workers, gamblers, and accusatory visitors alike.

I won't go back with them, but I can't allow them to beat Skelly senseless again.

Atel says, "Now, Medusa, I suppose it is necessary for us to blindfold you, no?"

I don't even respond.

"Look away from me, girl," Atel demands. He carefully removes my glasses and pulls a colorful sack over my moving hair and deadly eyes that less than an hour ago didn't turn the man in the bookstore to stone. Done, Atel snickers.

"What?" I ask.

He shoves me and punches me hard in the stomach. I stumble backwards into some crates, which cause me to fall forward onto my knees. I put my arms out and catch myself. But, wearing the hood, I can't breathe. I'm trying to take a breath, but my face and hair feel so warm they might actually catch fire.

I hear Skelly shouting, "Let her go! Let her be!"

Then there's silence so that I wonder what's happening.

Still snickering, Atel steps on my fingers. "Now doesn't that hurt, Medusa? You hear me, Medusa? This is what Rictus wants us to call you from now on. See, Maia is gone. Medusa, you are merely an animal now. And guess what, animal? We are attempting to save your sorry life. Good Thespula Dalton, our resident fortune teller, warned us that you might very well drown today. She had a dream where she saw you getting pulled downwards. Do you see, Medusa? We're here to change your future. We only seek to look out for you."

I'm breathing heavily, trying to stay calm even as I feel my anger rise.

Horst says, "Child, let this be a lesson. Whenever you leave, I will come to get you. It's the way things are."

"Shut up," I tell him, panting like a runner.

He laughs, big and strong, as if he's at a party.

"You're just a dumb Nazi," I say, my hair searching against the interior of the bag around my head. It wants Horst. It wants to hurt him even more than it wants to hurt Atel.

A wave of predatory desire washes over me.

I growl.

"Heal doggy," Atel says.

I leap at his voice and am on him in an instant. He nearly collapses backwards as I scratch his cheeks. The pythons of my hair shred the hood over my head into pieces, and I see that Atel appears frightened. His hands are empty and searching, as if he wants to find an exit. There's a wooden pallet beside me and I lift it and swing it about, striking Atel in his privates, which sends him to the ground in a heap, which is something funny to me about men. Why does that hurt so much?

Instantly, I leap at Horst, who has leveled his pistol on me. We collide and he covers his eyes. While he bangs against my back with the side of his gun, it fires randomly, just missing Skelly. With hardly an effort, my hair takes it from him and launches it up and over the mountainous flats. Then I ensnare his arms and constrict them painfully. The other locks jerk his large head down to my rising knee, creating a resounding crack and causing him to topple like I hit him with an American baseball bat, even though I don't know how to play baseball.

I bend forward menacingly and start to crawl like a multi-legged spider in his direction.

Then I'm tackled from the side.

Willem's weight and momentum drive me into a tall pile of flats, throwing a few off the top and breaking others so that the whole thing seems on the verge of falling over. Somehow, Willem's tackle momentarily short circuits my brain. Then, shaking the hit off, I twist about, and stare into Willem's dimwitted eyes.

He looks like our collision shocked him, too. Then he smiles. "Your eyes are doing something funny," he tells me like we're friends. "They got the clouds in them." Grinning, he cocks a fist to batter me senseless, but as he stands there, first his fingers, then his hands and arms turn an ashen gray. Slowly, a new and sudden weight pulls them down to his side.

I pull my gaze away.

Willem moans, confused. He cocks his head and looks down at both of his hands. "Maia!" he suddenly squeals. "Something's wrong. Help me, please, 'cause it hurts!"

I hiss at him.

He says, "That's not nice."

I move away, to where Horst is alone. I need to inflict pain upon the man who has made a point of inflicting it on me.

"I'm injured, Maia," he informs me.

"Horst, look at me!" I demand, reaching for him. But he won't make eye contact. I walk down his back like a spider, and breathe over his shoulder. I turn his head playfully so that if he opens his eyes, he'll turn to stone, too. Then, as if I'm looking down at the scene from above, I realize what I'm doing, and I'm sickened. Standing, I stagger away.

Skelly says, "Jesus, Joseph, and Mary, child." He crosses

himself as he holds my suitcases and glasses.

Willem, who still appears confused, and Atel, who's still moaning, watch us leave.

10
THE MURKY DARKNESS

Rushing out from the stack of crates, we walk as fast as Skelly can go toward the docks, where large trucks rumble past beside forklifts, and enormous wooden crates are stacked three high. We move past construction and men working on engines the size of houses. I look at my sunglasses, but I don't put them on. After my encounter with Horst, Atel, and Willem, I've come to understand that anger is the mechanism that slowly turns men to stone.

I glance over at him. Speaking of anger, I'm still angry with Skelly. At the same time, he's the only person who's ever been nice to me, and I love him for that. "Skelly, who… who am I?"

"Just a young woman who needs to leave her past behind."

I can't argue or respond to that, because it's true, only I don't feel very young.

We see Pier 19 ahead and hurry through an enormous storage warehouse that looks like it should simply fall down. It's dark inside, the metal tresses covered in rust and cobwebs, debris on the floor, and the air heavy with the smell of dampness. It probably hasn't been used since before the war. We see an enormous sliding wall open as if to take in crane loads of supplies, and we head out onto the deck of the pier, where the large, gray Sunderland Traveler has pulled away.

Anxious, Skelly hurries to the edge of the concrete dock and peers over the long edge, looking for something. He moves to our right and signals to me. "Hurry now, Maia. She ain't gone, yet."

Overhead, the freighter's massive engines are pumping dark exhaust into the cold blue sky. Skelly scrambles down a latter that is bolted to the pier. He jumps onto a floating, rectangular metal platform not eight or so meters from the ship's gang plank. Skelly screams at the ship, "Hey! Hey, up there!"

A sailor looks over the side and calls to us, "Ya must be Skelly!"

"That's me, me boy, and I got ya one more passenger, courtesy of Captain Sweeny! Can ya throw me a line, lad?"

"Sure'n," the guy calls back.

Skelly unhooks us from the pier and shoves us away so that we float out over the dark water. To me, he explains, "They use these floats for painting the hulls of ships, dear. They're everywhere around these docks."

I nod, wondering if he was once a shoreman. Then a rope comes twirling down from the deck, landing with a bump beside my foot. I look up to see the sailor tying the rope off so that we can pull ourselves over. Leaning down, Skelly starts hauling us toward the gang plank with one hand. The other must be sore from one of the scuffles he'd been involved in over the last two days. All the while, a set of tugs slowly goes about repositioning themselves around the ship.

I blurt, "I don't want to go."

Skelly continues pulling. "Ya got yourself a new life coming up, don't ya know? A… a whole new world with your ma and pa." He stops to catch his breath. "And them nice little houses with them cute little American backyards. Person can be anything they wants to be."

Slowly, we move closer to the ship, and with every meter, I wonder if leaving Europe and the Festival de Tordré will truly allow me to start again. Can running away change who I am? Can anything?

"Maia, listen," Skelly calls at me. "Captain Sweeny, he's taking five thousand dollars for his troubles. With it, he'll give ya passage and get ya past American port security. Ya will be left with eighty-seven thousand dollars US, dear. I counted."

I nod. I don't really have a sense for how much that is.

"When ya get to the states, tell the police who ya are, but don't tell them about the money. Tell them your story, but keep the money to yourself."

"Okay…" I start to say, but I'm cut short by an explosion, like a missile has struck the back of our float.

Instantly, the entire platform heaves high in the front and dips underwater in the back, so that I worry it might actually roll over like a domino on its tall end. A wave of dirty water washes over me and Skelly as we tumble down painfully. After a frightening second, the float rights itself, and I roll over and face the back of the platform, where I find myself staring at two ashen gray, immobile hands grappling for a hold.

Confused, I scoot forward. "Willem?" I say.

"Maia," he coughs, trying to gain a grip with fingers that don't work. "I'm supposed to kill you guys… Okay? That's what Horst said. I got to or I can't go back to Mother. So I got to."

I stare at him.

"Help me," he says.

"Leave him!" Skelly spats furiously, as he resumes pulling us toward the ship.

"We can't just let him go," I holler.

"Ya heard why he's here!"

I grab and hold onto one of Willem's stone hands.

Skelly says, "I'll get him when ya are safe on board, not before."

I look up to see if the sailor is still on deck, but he's not. I realize that the gang plank is lowering and figure he's working a wench somewhere.

I peer back at Willem.

"Please, Maia."

"Please what?" I ask him. "Save you so you can kill us?"

"Yeah... Okay? Do you mind?"

I almost smile at him, which would be cruel. It's such a revealing comment, though. Willem has no idea what killing is or means. Maybe he thinks it's sleep. Maybe he believes it's a trip or a conversation with a priest. I don't know. No matter, he has no idea how others fear death just as much as he does.

"Help me," he says like a child. "Ya gotta help me!" he begs over and over, scrambling with hands that refuse to work.

We bump against the huge freighter's hull, which causes Willem to slip. His frozen fingers just catch on a dented area of the float.

I ensnare Willem with my tresses. Situating myself, I pull back with the full strength of my locks and body. Skelly says to me, "What're ya doing, Maia? I'll get him in a minute."

"We need to save him now."

"Listen, sweetie, when the gangplank is down, ya gots to get on it. Ya won't have any time for that bastard!"

"Then help me, 'cause I'm not leaving him!"

Skelly curses, ties off the rope, and rushes over, grabbing one of Willem's coarse, stone arms. We pull, but we can't get him out of the water. It's like two people trying to lift a solid block of marble.

"What kind of blasted pants ya wearing, Willem?" Skelly jokes sarcastically, his teeth gritted so that I can hear the enamel on them grind like train wheels.

Willem says, "Just normal pants. I weigh a lot on account of my new stone feet and legs."

At that, I nearly release him. I'm horrified. My heart stumbles and kicks awkwardly for a moment. Somehow, my eyes turned whole sections of his big body to rock. How? How could it be?

Willem smiles and says, "Maia, you remember when I… I tried to cut your hair off and you didn't want me to. We kind of arm wrestled over the razor 'til you got mad and hurt me. That… that was funny, wasn't it?"

Like a flood, the memory comes back to me. Until this moment, I'd forgotten the details of that distant afternoon. I can see him now, an old fashioned razor in his hand, that frightening, blank grin on his face. He'd come to shave the living, feeling hair off of my head. He had grabbed me and held me in his thick arms, and I had fought back. How could I have forgotten such a thing? I'd allowed everyone in the festival to pin his intellectual problems on an uncontrollable evil inside of me. "Yes, it was funny," I tell him, because if he slips under, I want him to go in peace. There's no reason to hold it over him now.

"Yeah," he agrees, and the waves from the tugboat's wake wash into the float, rocking it wildly.

"You're gonna be okay," I tell him.

"Maia, it's real nice you're gonna save me," he says, but his voice wavers, and I wonder if he is scared I actually won't. Then, in an instant, Willem is gone.

So that I'm not pulled in after him, my hair releases him to the depths.

I lean forward and watch him slide quickly downward. He disappears into the murky darkness like a giant, weighted jellyfish, his clothes puffing outward as he drops away. "No!" I scream, my locks reaching for him. I turn to Skelly. "We need to save him!"

Skelly blinks and wraps his arms around me as we kneel atop the unstable float. "I can't child. Ya felt him, it'd take a crane to pull him up. It'd take a blasted crane."

I hear the gangplank's wench stop. I hear the sailor clang down the metal treads. At the bottom, he says to me, "Quick, girly!" He extends an arm, and I realize he wants to help me on board. "It's now or never," the guy says, his accent not so different from Skelly's.

I watch the swirling water for what seems like a long time, wishing it was me instead of Willem. How could it be that I'd never forgiven him his cruelty on the grounds that he was simply slow? He had the intelligence of a child?

The Sunderland Traveler begins to move very slowly away from us, and the sailor says, "Jump now or stay behind."

Skelly lurches over painfully. He presses my suitcases against me. "These're important. Don't lose them, dear. They will be your freedom from want."

I take them by the handles.

"No hesitation," Skelly tells me. "Your life is ahead, not behind."

I look at his battered face, at the urgency in his blood shot eyes, and a jolt of fear erupts from the thunder clouds of my soul. How can I leave? Who will know where Willem's body is? Will Thespula blame me for his disappearance? Will she think I killed him somehow? And, I can't help but wonder if I did. Somewhere inside, did I know what my gaze could do? If so, shouldn't I be the one who drown? Shouldn't his innocence have won over my evil?

Then, selfishly I worry for myself. I can't help it. My future is so blank. Ahead of me, everything is scattered. If I actually go, how will I make my way in America? Will I end up alone in that strange country, with its cities and deserts and countless roads that pass over lakes the size of oceans, waterfalls like moving glaciers, and mountains that rise upwards as if entire chunks of the moon have fallen to earth? Will I be alone in a land full of cactus, canyons, and redwood trees that brush the clouds, a land that sweeps and sweeps and sweeps away till it reaches the Pacific Ocean clear on the other side of the world? Will I know what to do in supermarkets larger than circus tents, that contain anything anyone could ever want, or will I just wander, helplessly?

Sharply, Skelly says, "Maia!"

But my mind just keeps reeling. How does a person find a place to live in America? How do they travel or get around. What if I can't go looking for my parents because I don't have a passport? And what if I can't ever find them since I don't even know how to begin looking?

Exasperated, Skelly jumps onto the metal stairway and holds out a hand. "Maia, let's go, me and you," he says.

My hair clicks angrily in my ears, and I slowly regain my focus. The ship is in front of me, the gangplank's platform is drifting farther and farther away. Skelly is leaning over the empty space between, holding out his hand.

Feeling numb with sadness, I reach for it and step off the float.

"Up we go," the sailor says, and Skelly and I stumble after him to the deck of the ship, where he goes into a room and presses the motor to bring the gangplank up. The ship begins to move farther from the shore, but I keep my eyes on the drifting black float and the spot where Willem disappeared. I wonder if there isn't something I can do, if there isn't some way to save him. No one deserves to die that way.

Skelly says to me. "He was gone when he jumped. He should've never left shore."

I can't speak.

He touches my back, and I don't pull away. "If there was something we could've done, we'd have done it. But even if we'd located a crane, he would've died by the time we fished him out."

I keep my eyes on the spot. I keep looking till we're out in the channel and around the bend, moving gently along the Rhine River, towards the Netherlands and then out into the North Sea.

SWEPT AWAY

We're a week out of Köln, and I continue to have nightmares. In them, poor Willem drowns, again and again. Again and again, he says, "Thanks, Maia. It's nice you're gonna save me." Then he's gone. I don't save him. I never save him. Worse, because of me, he's crippled. He can't use his hands or his feet, can't grasp or kick or struggle to survive. Because of me, he weighs thousands of kilos, he's both man and rock.

Awakening from my third bad dream of the evening, I try not to stir Skelly. He's been sick during most of the trip so far. Plus, there're quite a few rats living aboard the Sunderland Traveler, and they visit with me at night. We have an audience of dirty rodents every night from midnight till morning. Like a tiny choir, they mass at the edge of the light and watch me sleep or read. It's sort of cute. But Skelly, who's slept under trailers, in mud, and atop dirt and stone, is so scared of them he climbs on top of his bed like a little old lady when they're around. So I tell them to leave before he awakens.

Climbing from my cot, I lean down and whisper, "Run away, and don't frighten Skelly. He's sick enough."

They hesitate.

"Run, please," I beg.

After they leave, I go up on deck, where I sit on a storage hold cover and breathe in the cold air.

The ship's engines have been breaking down. Because of them, we've been plowing toward the port of New York City at about the same speed Christopher Columbus sailed across the Atlantic. I'm glad. I feel like I need the time to understand the changes that have taken place and the fact that I might actually get to meet people who were once my parents.

Shortly, Skelly finds me. Shivering dramatically, looking yellow, sweaty, and nauseous, he sits down and lets out a gasp. "Ya must've asked your furry friends to go away, huh?"

"I did."

"I appreciate that, dolly."

"It's easy to do," I assure him. "They don't mean to scare you."

"Yeah, sure." He shifts and groans. It's only been seven days since he was battered by Horst, Atel, and Willem, and he's still in pain. He holds up his trembling hands. "The bloody lack of booze is still biting my butt."

"I know," I say softly. "Maybe when we get to shore, you should just quit drinking alcohol so it doesn't happen again. Have you considered that?"

He looks off. "I don't want to promise ya nothing. I don't want ya to be let down with me any more."

I smile at him. "You mean, more than I already have been?"

"Yeah, that's what I mean."

I look out at the dark and distant horizon. The ocean is beautiful and mysterious, but, somehow, I miss the German countryside, the distant mountains and the heavy forests like a world of dampness. I also miss the rugged French landscapes and the dry, baked look of Italy. Because I might never see any of it again, I miss it all. I wasn't born in Europe, and I don't speak the languages, but I feel more European than American, and I think I always will.

I whisper softly to him, "Have you considered what we're leaving behind?"

"I have," Skelly says to me. "I have, and with every mile I feel cleaner."

I look over. "What do you mean?"

He wipes sweat from his brow. "Just that Rictus had a way of making me feel filthy. And more than anything else, we're leaving that jackal in our past, ain't we?"

I nod. "He made me feel that way, too."

"It was a talent." Skelly waits a few minutes, then he says, "Maia, what got ya up so early, girl?"

I consider lying but I don't. "Bad dreams."

"Ah, bad dreams. Let me guess, Willem?"

"Yeah."

"Maia, dear… love. I'm going to say the same thing I've been saying because it requires it till you understand the situation by heart. What happened to Willem wasn't your fault. Ya didn't ask him to follow us down the pier. He did it on orders from Horst or Atel. They made him who he was, and who he was is what caused him to drown that way. You didn't leave him. They left him."

Reflections from the moon wash a pale light over the vibrating steel deck. I can hear chains rattling off toward the bow.

Skelly adds, "Thank God for the one gift ya had no one could take away."

"What's that?"

"Resilience. Mental toughness. You've needed every bit of it."

Quietly, I try to change the subject. "When I get to America, I don't want to work in a cage."

He grins. "That's it? That's all you're hoping for?"

"For now."

"And your folks?"

"I don't know." I hesitate. "Until a week ago, I always thought they were Greek and poor and living on an island in the Aegean Sea. Now I find out my father's in the American military... or he was at least. It's been so long, I have no memory of them, and, probably, they forgot me. That's the truth."

"When you stand in their door, they'll know who you are. They'll be swept away with joy."

I stare off, thinking about that. Swept away with joy? It sounds so wonderful. Swept away. It sounds like the bad parts of my past can disappear.

My hair sways above me while Skelly shivers alongside. I am amazed by the speed of change in my life, a life that seemed frozen in routine and shackled by the whims of Rictus. Change occurs faster than I ever thought possible.

I get up and walk over to the side of the ship. I peer down at the water. During daylight, I like watching dolphins diving in front of the bow, but all I can see at night are distant reflections.

Skelly follows me and says, "In America, you can be anything you want to be."

"Anything?" I ask, smiling distantly.

"That's what they say."

"Then I want be human."

"And ain't that what ya are, dear?"

"Lately, the human part of me hasn't been all that obvious."

"Ah, come on. I've known a lot of women who lose their temper now and then. It's normal."

I grin. What's been happening to me is so much worse than losing my temper, and he knows it. "Maybe it's not the same,"

I say.

Skelly hunches forward and locks his hands together, weaving his fingers into a tiny basket. "Maia, love, don't overlook what's going on here. Now ya know who ya are and who ya are not. Dear, that's huge. You've never been sure before."

I don't know what he means.

Skelly watches me. He must recognize my confusion because he continues speaking. "Now ya know your parents didn't ever try to get rid of ya. They was also all human and loved ya and wanted ya and the only thing that happened was ya was taken from them. Doesn't that change things? Doesn't that change it all?"

Endless, rolling ocean waves rhythmically wash the ship's hull like someone shushing us over a loud speaker. I think about what he's said, and I'm surprised to find that his comments nearly cause me to cry.

I've been trying to come to terms with the fact that what never was can never be, and what was can never change. And there's a good and bad to both of those ideas. I am not who I believed myself to be. My parents were human, so I'm more girl than monster. However, I'm a girl who has thought herself a monster for years. That has a terrible effect. What happened so long ago, in a small German town, to an Air Force officer's daughter, to that man's wife, has altered the lives of everyone involved in different ways. But knowing the truth and how I came to The Festival de Tordré gives me slight peace of mind. In America, where people can be anything they want to be, maybe I can become anything, too. Despite my freakish qualities, my life no longer has to be limited to a sideshow career as Medusa's Daughter.

Skelly wipes back his hair and smiles. "Maia Gasol, I believe ya are going to do fine in this world. That's the way I feel in me heart. You'll find happiness."

I nod and hold tight to the Sunderland Traveler's metal rail. I can feel it tremble beneath my hands, the engines deep inside the ship sending tiny shockwaves up through the countless layers of steel as the propeller pushes us farther from home. It's confusing to hear him use my last name. It's also wonderful. I'm not normal, but I am somebody, somebody real. I put a hand on top of one of his. It takes me a moment, then I tell him, "Skelly, neither one of us is who we were anymore. We're both leaving our pasts behind."

He bites at a fingernail and gnaws it for a moment. "Aye, Maia, and good riddance to them both."

I close my eyes and nod gently. I hear the sound of gulls overhead, the conversations of sailors somewhere mid-ship, and the gentle movement of my living hair as it adjusts to the breeze. Softly, I say, "Goodbye past."

Special thanks: *Robert and Joyce Parke, Hank Young and Ann Boulton, Charley Levine and family, Lisa Coleman, Michael Van Huffel, Jeff Springer and Custom Model Railroads, Kim Lawler, Bob Cicero (Globe Poster), Debbie Rich at Digital Anarchy, Alan Greenberg, Cathy Evans (Shoot the Moon), Ninth Life, Jerry Dadds & Brook Yeaton, German deli place, Ozzie the cat, Frank and Gayle Murray, Kait Ciuchta, Johnny Fox, Jules Smith, Bertha's on Broadway, Captain Mike Schneider and the John Brown Liberty ship, Jack Gerbis and the Maryland Film Office, Kevin Perkins, Leslie F. Miller, Joe Giordano.*

Thank you to our Kickstarter Supporters: *Toné Compito Wellington, Ben & Valerie Margolin, St Paul Peterson, Dan, Terri, John and Carly Hobson, Michael and Eileen Crocetti, The Souper Freak Food Truck, Kemil, Yanis and Mohamed Gaouaoui, Dawn Runion, tiag® (The Informatics Applications Group), Stephen Cordova (NewPhidias), ValleyTone, Square One Entertainment.*

Jonathon, aka Scott, Fuqua wants to profoundly and humbly thank the same vital and caring people as Steve Parke as well as a few special individuals who showed faith, patience, and the ability to see when he couldn't, know when he couldn't, and—without question—envision when his vision failed. First, he thanks the crushingly talented Steve Parke for his—at times exhausted and at times tireless—work to find a way to make our work work. He thanks Steve's kindly wife for being tolerant beyond measure. He thanks his own beautiful, loving, funny, and very time-consuming family, Elegant Julie, Charming Calla, and Effervescent Gabriel, for consuming his time with things that brought happiness, contentment and pride in the midst of the odyssey that eventually saw this concept to completion. What would he do without them? Well, not much of anything worth mentioning. He'd like to thank his calm and caring mother, unintentionally humorous step-father, his very best siblings, brother Clay and sister Kate, and their generous and eccentric families. He'd like to extend thanks to his special (in a good way) in-laws, Jim and Sue and their massive extended family, all of whom continued to talk to him during visits, vacations, and holidays as he tried to explain what the hell he was attempting to do but hardly could. He'd like to thank his longtime, cynical, and faithful friend Hank Young for being

Hank, and his wife Ann for being who she is and not Hank, though Hank is not such a bad thing to be. Hank is Hank, and Scott would have it no other way. He'd like to thank Steve's parents, specifically for grinning in the face of what seemed like disaster and never spitting on him, though he would've if he'd been them. He'd like to thank his close friends, Glenn and Marian, Michael and Beth, Paul and Lauren, Anita and Josh, Paul and Cissy, Lanny and Teddy, Dennis and Carol, Babs and… well, everyone, and I mean everyone, he leaned on, moaned to, and cried in front of to get this thing out the door. He wants to thank Lauren Marks for lending her modelesque beauty and great air of mystery to the task of being Maia, and his own daughter, a mind-bogglingly powerful little actress—who isn't so little anymore—for being the young Maia. He thanks Doug for just about being as cool as a person can be and stitching, with his chiseled features and good humor, the scenes together. He gives a shout out to the psychologist who kept him together through a nanometer of thick and a thousand miles of thin. He wants to thank Susan for being a brilliant book designer and also dealing with two lunatics so well. And, of course, he thanks anyone and everyone who participated in the process of making these varied stories, contributing their likenesses, their time, their life, their money, and a lot of goodwill to this work. Scott is tired and bent, somewhat broken, but always assisted back to a standing position by so many infinitely generous people. It is beyond his meager ability to express his appreciation.